THE CORNER OF 1700 HAMILTON

VANIA RHEAULT

Created with Vellum

ALSO BY VANIA RHEAULT

Available from Coffee & Kisses Press

The Corner of 1700 Hamilton

Summer Secrets Novellas 1-3
Summer Secrets Novellas 4-6

Don't Run Away
Chasing You
Running Scared

Wherever He Goes

All of Nothing

The Years Between Us

His Frozen Heart
His Frozen Dreams
Her Frozen Memories
Her Frozen Promises

To my family and friends
who lose me every time I start a new story.

1700 Hamilton

CHAPTER ONE

"Rough day?"

Ben Langdon looked up from the polished oak of the bar top and stared blankly at the bartender. "What?" he asked.

The bartender slid a lowball glass of whiskey across the bar. "Rough day?"

Rough day. Fuck that. How about a rough month? Rough year. Rough life. "You could say." He reached behind him to pull his wallet from his dress jacket hanging on the back of his barstool, but the bartender shook his head.

"On the house," he said and continued to wipe down the spotless bar top with a dry white terrycloth rag.

Ben jerked a shoulder in thanks and resumed his study of the shining wood under the dim lights of the bar. If the bartender was going to let him drink for free, he wouldn't complain.

He'd never been to this bar before, and he'd noticed it for the first time today on his way home from work. Maybe he'd never been unhappy enough to notice the little hole in the wall that was actually a very nice Irish pub on the inside. Maybe God knew he needed some peace and quiet since he was the only patron in the entire bar on a Friday night at nine.

Ben appreciated the silence, sitting undisturbed, except for the chatty bartender.

The typical flat screen TV mounted above the bar was set to C-SPAN of all channels, and an old woman, her face full of pancake makeup and sporting bright pink lips, yammered on about something, her lips forming words but to no avail as the TV was muted and the closed captioning disabled.

"Wanna talk about it?"

"Not much to talk about . . . Danny," Ben said, squinting at the bartender's gold nametag pinned to his black vest. A blood red tie was knotted expertly beneath the bartender's throat, the white shirt popping against the black and red, the collar crisp.

He was handsome, if men studied other men, the way women studied other women.

Ben had heard that once. Women dressed for each other, not men. To show off, to feel better about themselves. Did men do that? He sat, his shoulders hunched, his elbows resting on the edge of the bar. He studied the bartender, taking in the dress shirt, the tie, the vest. *Nah.* When he'd dressed this morning he hadn't thought about other men. He'd thought about *her*, and if she would have recommended the red and grey striped tie or the grey and black.

Nope, men dressed for women and women dressed for women. Maybe he would look for a woman who would dress for him. He would go shopping with her, help her choose dresses. Dresses that would look good in a heap on his bedroom floor.

Maybe he was drunk.

"Something has you down and out," Danny commented, leaning against the bar.

Ben shrugged and looked above Danny's head. The woman's mouth was still moving but now she held a small white . . . poodle. The bottom of the screen read: *Audrina Prescott, Animal Rights Activist.*

Huh.

How many rabbits had sacrificed their little fluffy lives testing Audrina Prescott's bright pink lipstick?

His empty glass was replaced with new. Danny was trying to get him shitfaced. Did he want to drag his body into the back room, slit his throat, and leave him to rot behind a case of Pinot Grigio?

"My fiancée broke off our engagement," Ben admitted, the black jacket of his suit pulling uncomfortably across his shoulders. Had he gained weight? He didn't think so. Besides it wouldn't have gathered in shoulders; it would have collected in his gut.

He patted his stomach. Nope, still flat. If anything, he'd probably lost a little. He hadn't felt like eating much since Megan left.

Well, so what. There were plenty of mice in the pet store, or however the saying went. He would throw out a bit of cheese and snap one up, like a rat in a trap.

Snap!

Somehow that didn't seem right.

"That's tough."

"Not really."

Not when it came right down to it. She'd done him a favor. People who weren't in love had no business being together. Just because she'd been first to esc—er, leave, it was still a good thing.

3

He'd liked her. A lot. A whole lot. Living a life with her would have been a smooth, easy existence.

"No?"

Danny's black wavy hair was shining, his blue eyes crinkling in the corners, as if he were enjoying a joke Ben hadn't heard. He probably had a cute little girl tucked away somewhere, waiting for him to come home.

The little pub was decorated in blacks and dark browns, the colors giving off a soothing vibe beneath the orange glow of the muted lights.

Banquettes lined the opposite wall, huge U-shaped booths that could fit at least six people, though he couldn't imagine the bar being as busy as that.

There weren't any pool tables; there wasn't a dance floor. A couple of plants, but from this distance he didn't know if they were real or fake.

It was a small, cozy, quiet space. Every once in a while he caught the notes of a piano drifting through the speaker system. He was sitting toward the end of the bar, his sad reflection staring back at him in the mirrored wall behind the collection of liquor bottles.

Unless he was gay. Ben studied Danny in a new light. No. He didn't seem to be. He supposed it was too gauche to ask, and besides, Danny hadn't hit on him once while he'd been sitting here. Just kept sliding him drinks he didn't ask for, which was fine with him. He would pay for them, even if it meant tipping him a fifty on his way out the door.

"This place can't make much money," Ben told him now, rolling the glass that still held a finger of whiskey between his palms.

"I get by," Danny said, unconcerned, his eyes drifting toward the silent TV.

"You own—"

Ben's question was interrupted by a group of women bursting through the door, their laughter and bright dresses tearing through Ben's serenity like a jagged blade.

They brought with them the winter's chill, and he shivered as the wisps of cold air penetrated his suit coat.

The door bumped shut, and the group migrated to one of the banquettes, the women taking off their thick winter jackets and getting settled into the leather and wood booth.

They were laughing, their earrings glinting and their hair pinned up. They were dressed to be out on the town, and it puzzled Ben why the group chose the little Irish bar.

One of the women, after taking off her jacket and revealing a short cocktail dress, ran across the black tile and wedged herself between him and an empty stool. She propped herself onto the bar with her arms, her legs dangling.

Danny beamed and leaned over to give her a smacking kiss on the lips.

So this was Danny's woman, Ben thought with a tug of envy. She was gorgeous. Her shining black hair was pinned in a mass of riotous curls at the crown of her head, displaying a huge floppy bow at the back of her neck, the ends streaming down her back. Her dress was an emerald green, short, and sleeveless, revealing her toned arms that were now steadying herself against the bar, her stomach pressed against the edge.

"You're here for the party then, lass." Danny switched to an Irish brogue and Ben smiled into his drink with amusement.

It must have amused the woman too because she laughed out loud. "Yes! You know it's Brigid's bachelorette party."

VANIA RHEAULT

"Aye. Brigid. A fine young lad finally captured her heart."

The woman giggled again.

Heat pooled in Ben's belly, and he started to get hard. That wasn't good. The last thing he needed was to fall for a woman already taken. Deciding to cut his losses, he started to put on his jacket.

"You're not leaving us already? You oughtn't leave me alone with this group!" Danny protested, the hint of brogue coloring his speech. He hadn't noticed it before, and now he didn't know if it was real or for show.

For the first time since Megan left, Ben smiled. "That isn't a hardship."

The woman met his eyes, and it was as if time stood still. Even as the clichéd thought ran through his head, his breathing shallowed and his heart hammered. Her green eyes sparkled against the green of her dress, fringed bangs and long black eyelashes accenting them, giving her a wide-eyed, innocent look. Cold still lingered on her skin, the apples of her cheeks flushing prettily, and her lips sparkled with some kind of lipgloss.

Danny looked between then, smirking.

"Hi."

"Hello," he said, surprised his voice was so smooth. He needed to get out of there before he embarrassed himself.

The woman still hung on the bar and she started to swing her legs back and forth, the toes of her silver heels banging against the wood.

Swing, bang, swing, bang.

Danny waved the terrycloth rag between them. "This is . . ."

He hadn't given Danny his name, though he'd pilfered the bartender's from his nametag. "Benjamin. Ben." He

6

held out his hand, and she settled her feet on the gold footrest that ran along the bottom of the bar near the floor. She took his hand. Hers was still cold; she must not have been wearing gloves.

Extracting her hand from his, she leaned over and cupped his face in her chilly palms. "I bet you were a Benji in school."

Appalled, Ben blushed and cleared his throat. "How did you know?"

"Because you are so freaking adorable!"

Breaking the mood, the women behind them started shouting. "Lila! Come on! We want the booze!"

"I'm coming!"

Lila moved away and immediately left Ben bereft. She stood near him, her feet still planted on the footrest, but she'd pulled her hands away from his face and he prickled with regret.

"So you came in to use me for me booze," Danny lamented, his brogue thickening with mock despair.

"You knew we were planning on coming in," Lila told him, grinning.

"Aye," Danny agreed mournfully.

"This doesn't seem the best place to party." Ben snapped his mouth shut, embarrassed he butted into their conversation. Danny probably needed the money and wanted his girlfriend to bring in her friends.

"Oh, it's not," Lila agreed, nodding her head. "But Danny told us to come in for a couple bottles, and I can never say no to him."

"I wanted the company." Danny winked conspiratorially at Ben, though Lila saw it and shook her head in amusement.

Danny grabbed the alcohol of choice for Lila and her

friends, and again Ben attempted to slip on his jacket. He felt a tug of sadness he would probably never see Lila again, but he'd never made it a habit to encroach on someone else's territory and he wouldn't start now. Besides, they seemed like a happy couple.

"Don't go yet." She wiggled onto the barstool next to him. She leaned sideways, her elbow on the bar, her head propped in her hand, and she rested the other hand on the back of her barstool. She crossed her legs. "How did you find this place?"

Surprised she was making conversation, he settled his black wool jacket into place on the back of his own stool and shrugged. "I was walking home from work and here it was. Decided to pop in for a minute and here I am." He paused, trying to find a tactful way to approach a subject that was none of his concern. "It doesn't seem as if this place gets much business."

Though it didn't seem as if either of them were hurting for money, Ben felt a bit indignant on Lila's part. Danny should be able to take care of his woman properly. Being a bartender in a dead bar didn't seem to be doing the job, at least, in Ben's opinion.

She laughed. "We do all right," she commented as Danny popped corks on three champagne bottles at the booth where the other women were sitting, flutes in hand.

The ladies hooted as foam covered their table.

"You're missing all the action," Ben said reluctantly. He didn't want her to go.

"So I am," she agreed, "but the night is young, and I'm afraid I have many hours of this to go."

"You don't like to party?"

"Not so much," she admitted, smiling at her friends as Danny poured champagne all around. "But it's a special night for Brigid, though, and we started here to, ah, prime the pump, as you say, for free. Danny won't charge us for the bottles."

"He's a nice guy."

Ben *did* think the bartender was a decent sort, slipping him lowball glasses for free. He tucked the idea into the back of his mind to pay for the women's champagne too. It was the least he could do for a woman who caught his eye. Even if she wasn't available.

Lila held out her hand. "It was nice meeting you. Don't be a stranger, Ben."

Ben frowned as Lila slipped off the barstool to join her friends. She slid into the banquette and picked up a flute to take a sip.

While women laughed and talked, he grabbed his jacket to tug it on and head home. He bought a little house not long after Megan said yes to his proposal. The three bedroom house was located in a quiet neighborhood not far from an elementary school. Whenever he had thought about their children, he'd always pictured his and Megan's children blonde, like her. Now, for a brief second, he saw a little girl with pigtails, black, like her mother's hair.

He shook his head. He had barely met the woman, she was taken, either a girlfriend or a wife, and he had no business staying here any longer.

"You're really going to leave me here with that bunch?"

Danny would have made a good friend. Maybe he would come back sometime. "I think you'll be okay." His eyes locked on Lila, but she was speaking with one of her friends and didn't see him looking at her.

He adjusted his jacket, reached for his wallet, and he took out a hundred dollar bill, pushing it across the bar. "Have a good night, Danny," he said, nodding a goodbye.

Danny rubbed the bill between his index finger and thumb and frowned, puzzled.

Too far away now to say anything, Ben cocked his head toward Lila's table and shrugged at Danny's suppressed smile before he slipped out the door into the cold night's air.

Cold wind bit into his cheeks and he missed the touch of Lila's palms when she'd cupped his face between her small hands.

A little thing. A woman who could curl into a ball on his lap, his arms easily encircling her. He pictured them watching a movie, sitting that way, or maybe holding her while she was tired and she drifted to sleep, her head on his shoulder.

It surprised him he was so taken with her. Megan was a willowy ash blonde and his girlfriend before her had possessed similar coloring. He didn't know what it was about Lila that spoke to him, but he'd barely met her and he missed her spark, her effervescence. He hoped she'd be all right partying tonight.

He was about to call a cab instead of braving the elements when his phone rang. Amazed he'd heard the faint chime over the wind rushing in his ears, he stepped into a brick alcove that housed the entrance for a bookstore closed for the night.

The number came up unknown, but he felt compelled to answer it, and the temperature was too damn cold to argue with himself over the decision. "Yeah?"

". . . Need your help."

Static filled the line, and Ben didn't recognize the voice. "What?" he yelled into his cell phone, huddling into the doorway to protect himself from the wind. He plugged his ear with his finger. "What?"

"Need your help!"

The voice was clearer this time, but he still had no idea who'd called.

"Who is this? Where are you?" he shouted.

He wasn't about to turn down a friend who needed his help, and he didn't want to go home anyway. He didn't want to face the empty house.

Well, not entirely empty. Megan had left her cat behind. She'd asked him if he would keep Tabby, or Tabitha, if she was being naughty, and he reluctantly agreed.

The little black cat had taken to him and besides having to keep the litter box clean and buy the little furball food, she was no trouble.

Ben had asked Megan why she hadn't wanted to keep Tabby, and the truth had come out, albeit unwillingly. Megan's new boyfriend was allergic to cats and rather than trying to find her a new home, it was easier for Ben just to keep her.

He hated the thought of Megan hooking up behind his back. True, he worked a lot—who didn't these days—but the knowledge she'd been cheating made him sad, and for a moment his eyes pricked with emotion.

Or it could have been because it was goddamn cold outside.

He didn't think Lila was the type of woman who would do that to a man. He bet she read a book while she waited for Danny to come home after a long night at the pub.

"We're at—"

Another burst of static cut off the caller.

"Where?" he shouted over the buzz and the winter wind at his back.

"*1700 Hamilton.*"

He almost missed the address before the line went dead.

The bright screen told him the call had lasted a brief thirty-four seconds, and he pressed the phone icon to call the number back.

"The number you have dialed has been changed, disconnected, or is temporarily not in service. If you feel you have reached this recording in error, please check the number and try your call again or call customer service for assistance. Message 6791T."

What the hell.

He couldn't ignore the call now. If the guy he talked to thought he was calling him for rescue and he didn't do anything . . .

1700 Hamilton. That wasn't far from him, and he could always use a little adventure.

Well, maybe not, but despite his misgivings, he started in the opposite direction from where he'd come. He stopped in front of The Lucky Clover, the Irish bar where he'd met Lila.

Better to cut it off now, he thought, and he kept walking, wishing like hell if he stepped back inside that little bar Lila would jump from the banquette and run straight into his arms.

He had it bad, and it didn't make any sense at all.

Sleet mixed with the wind, and he knew without a doubt after this little escapade he'd be calling a cab to take him home. But even with the weather, he wasn't the only one on the downtown streets at ten-thirty at night.

A group of drunk twenty-something men stumbled by him and let themselves into The Lucky Clover. He hoped Danny wasn't in for a load of trouble, though the boys didn't look it. Just a group out for a good time on a Friday night, much like Lila and her friends.

Shoving his hands into the pockets of his black winter

jacket, he continued on. He gripped his keys in one pocket, felt his phone and wallet in the other.

Where the hell was 1700 Hamilton, and what was it? He knew this city like the back of his hand, yet . . . all he knew for sure was that he was going in the correct general direction.

Goddamn, it was freezing outside.

He bet Lila was cold in her short dress and sandals. He wondered how long her hair was when it wasn't pinned up. He wondered how long she and Danny had been together. They'd had a familiarity about them he envied.

He and Megan had almost reached that point.

That was the best part of a relationship; it was probably why he proposed. When being with someone was still fresh, still new, but comfortable. Knowing favorite foods, restaurants, drinks, sleeping positions, movies, music, but with surprises. Oh, your grandmother lived in Oshkosh, my step-uncle's sister lives there now.

Ben's mouth quirked.

A tall grey stone building sat on the corner of the street, an alley running along its side. He'd walked straight into a bad part of the city. The tall streetlight that should have been shining was shot out, and the streets that had been full of people minutes ago were empty.

He was glad he didn't have his car with him because he sure as hell wouldn't have parked it on this street. Not if he wanted to find it in one piece ever again.

"Hey, buddy. C'mere."

In the alley, an old man leaned over a fire burning in an old oil barrel. It was almost as if the man had whispered in his ear, or he'd heard the old man's voice in his head.

Impossible.

He approached the man, too trusting to think of being

nervous or apprehensive. He was in decent shape anyway; he'd be able to defend himself against the guy if need be. "Can I help you?"

"I think that's my question." The old man warmed his hands over the fire.

Ben couldn't resist the warmth of the flames and held out his hands as the old man was, the heat thawing his fingertips. The alleyway provided a welcome shelter from the wind. "You want to help me?"

The old man's eyes glittered in the orange flames portraying intelligence and old, wizened soul. He was dressed in layers upon layers of dirty black clothing and looked as if he hadn't had a bath in weeks. He shouldn't be out in the cold like this, and Ben wanted to help him, take him somewhere or give him some cash so he could afford a warm and safe place to stay for the night.

"What's your name?"

The man's face was grizzled, his jaw covered in grey beard, his eyebrows bushy, his long hair peeking from beneath a black winter stocking hat. A flash of . . . sadness, perhaps, shadowed the old man's eyes, and for a second, Ben was sorry he asked.

"They call me Joe."

They call me Joe. The old man didn't know his own name, and that's what the other street people called him. Ben's throat closed in sympathy. "Do you have a place you can spend the night?"

"Oh, sure," Joe said, almost airily, as if he didn't worry where to lay his head on a nightly basis. "The Catholic church down the way will let me in. Father Tim is a good fella. I do a bit of work for him from time to time in exchange for a cot in the back."

Ben nodded. "That's good. You should head over there

soon. It's only going to get colder out here. I need to get going," he said, putting his hands in his pockets, fingering his wallet. "I got a call from someone saying they need my help." He paused. "Do you know where 1700 Hamilton is? Am I close?"

"You're looking at it." Joe tilted his head to the building behind him.

Great. He wasn't in the mood to go on some sort of strange journey. Through a sharp stab of guilt, he wished now he hadn't answered his phone.

The buzz from Danny's whiskey disappeared. In its place he felt tired, and, if he was honest, lonely. No, he didn't want to go home, but he sure as hell didn't want to find out what was happening at 1700 Hamilton either.

"What are you looking for, Ben?" Joe asked, rubbing his hands together over the heat, his stare steady.

Joe was asking figuratively, studying his face over the barrel fire, but he didn't know what he was looking for figuratively, or literally for that matter, and frankly, he didn't think now was the time to think about it.

It was getting late.

"My friends," Ben said, taking the easy way out.

He pulled his wallet out of his pocket. Ben always felt more secure when he carried cash, and tonight, it was paying off. "Here." Ben pushed two one hundred dollar bills into Joe's warm, dirty hand, along with his business card. "I want to help you, if you'll let me. Give me a call. Father Tim will let you use a phone."

Ben let his guard down for a moment. "I could use another friend."

Lila's smile and bright green eyes came to his mind and he was struck in the heart by how much he missed her, wanted her.

Maybe he should have . . .

No. He remembered Danny's friendliness, his sense of humor. He remembered the feeling of betrayal when he had learned of Megan's defection from their relationship. He would never do that to another person.

Joe pocketed the money and card and to his surprise, gave him a firm handshake. "You'll find what you're looking for, young man."

Ben appreciated the faith and the confidence, but he wasn't sure if he ever would. People spent their whole lives searching. Some people found what they needed and threw it away. Some people found what they needed but never realized it until they lost it. Some people gave up entirely.

He didn't know if he was any of those kinds of people, but he remembered the burn when he stared into Lila's eyes, and he vowed he wouldn't rest until he found a woman he could have, who wanted him in return.

Who wouldn't throw him away as Megan had.

"Thanks," Ben said, gripping Joe's hand. "Take care now and call me."

He pulled his hand from Joe's dry and steady grasp and stepped out of the alley. As the wind slapped him, he turned to wave at Joe once more, but the man was gone.

He stopped dead in his tracks. Ben hadn't introduced himself, yet Joe had known his name.

Jesus Christ.

He trudged against the wind and the tiny bits of frozen rain, trotted up the concrete stairs of the building, and stepped gratefully into the tastefully decorated lobby of 1700 Hamilton.

Music shook the floor.

A bouncer stood in the shadows. He was a hulk of a man, his hands folded in front of him. Bald and frowning, he wore a black shirt under a jacket that must have been tailored especially for him. When the bouncer failed to greet him or stop him from entering the dance club, he moved through the darkened lobby. Sconces were fastened to the paneled walls, a rich red carpet covered the floor.

A tall woman stood behind a counter, a large closet at her back. Her short hair was colored bright orange, and she wore perfectly matched lipstick. "Coat check?" she chirped, tugging at her black dress, the neckline dipping dangerously low. She wasn't wearing a bra.

He shook his head to decline; he didn't want to be here long enough to check his jacket.

"Suit yourself," she replied, smacking gum. She cackled at the obvious pun, then leaned over, her breasts spilling onto the counter.

Ben winced.

The woman laughed.

Chuckling, the bouncer watched the scene. "Don't mind Iris. Not unless you want what she's got."

What Ben wanted was a glass of whiskey while he sat in front of his fireplace, the cat in his lap.

"You're too much woman for me," he told her truthfully.

The bouncer let out a roar of laughter.

"I'd be gentle with you, doll baby," Iris teased, patting her breasts as if to make certain they were still attached to her body. "I bet you're a big boy."

Ben coughed. "Not as big as he is," he answered drolly, jerking his thumb at the bouncer, and he stepped closer to the two huge black doors that led to the inner workings of the club.

Iris barked, "He's not as big as you'd think, honey. But he likes to pretend he is."

The bouncer's protests were swallowed by the

pounding music as Ben heaved open one of the black doors by its ornate twisted iron handle.

"You shoulda checked your coat!" Iris yelled a moment before the door slammed shut behind him.

Ben did a double take, swallowing a huge ball of unease.

The door didn't have a handle on this side. In fact, the door blended into the wall, perfectly disguised.

There was no way getting out the way he came in.

His favorite Kill Hannah song thumped a violent beat, shaking the building. The bass rattled him, vibrating through his body all the way down to his toes.

A woman stood behind a squat black podium, and she crooked a finger asking him to come closer. "You should have checked your coat," she yelled.

Ben shrugged. He was about to move away when she grabbed his arm.

She rubbed her middle and forefinger against her thumb, and he gave her a fifty dollar bill. She grinned, her red lipstick almost black, her hair so black it gleamed blue in the club's flashing lights. She tucked the bill between her breasts which were cradled by a low-cut black corset and laughed, a devilish glint in her eyes, daring him to say something to her for not offering him change.

Because he damn well knew no cover would cost fifty bucks.

The hostess wiggled her fingers at him, but Ben leaned over the podium to yell in her ear, "I got a phone call from a friend who said he needed help. Do you know anything about that?" He didn't offer her any more money; she'd taken him for enough.

She stepped from behind the podium. She wore a black miniskirt so short her garter hooks and the tops of her black stockings were visible under the lace hem. Along one slim thigh a small, flat knife was tucked into the elastic of her stocking.

A Bond girl in the making, Ben thought, tamping down a smile. She had the curves, the fifty peeking from her corset around a swell of creamy white cleavage. Her waist was slim, her hips flared. Her calves curved sexily, aided by the sky high stilettos she wore on her little feet. His gaze traveled from her toes up to her kohl rimmed eyes, such a dark brown they appeared black, her hair cut into a sharp bob.

She smoothed her hand over his tie.

The hostess finally shook her head and answered Ben's question. "No trouble here."

Ben snorted, sure that wasn't the case. "Thanks."

He turned from the hostess to the club and leaned over the black waist-high railing.

It was similar to looking down from the top floor of a shopping center. The third, second, and bottom floors of the club were visible, with the huge circular dance floor located in the middle of the bottom floor. Three levels of booze, drugs, skin, and sin.

Ben knew where he was now and wished he hadn't come.

1700 Hamilton.

Ben had entered The Maze.

CHAPTER TWO

T hat explained the doors without handles.

The Maze's motto was "One way in. No way out." Which was ridiculous, of course. The Maze closed for the night like any other bar.

Ben checked his phone for the time. If he couldn't find his way out, he would be trapped for four hours. Jesus Christ.

He walked around the upper level, and the black metal grating allowed him to see the top of people's heads partying beneath his feet. His stomach lurched and he looked away. He'd never been good with heights.

The uppermost level contained little, and it seemed The Maze's clientele used the space as a reprieve from the crowds below.

He wove around people holding drinks of all sizes and colors, some sitting in lounge chairs popping with color taking a break from the frenzy of the floors below. The walls were bare but for the shiny black paneling that matched the back of the front door trapping its unsuspecting guests inside.

Unsuspecting, my ass. Ben was probably the one person in the whole city who hadn't cared when The Maze opened its doors. He hadn't listened to the gossip or the stories. Megan had wanted to try it, and he'd forced her to go with her friends instead.

He couldn't think of anything he wanted to be doing less.

The floor swayed queasily under his feet, and the stark interior lent the club a warehouse atmosphere. Black support beams crisscrossed the ceiling, flashing lights attached at all angles. Four floors. The building hadn't seemed big enough from the outside.

He followed the circular curve of the top floor to the lone staircase at the far end of the level.

His skin prickled with sweat. He should have checked his jacket. Dammit.

No, not dammit.

He probably wouldn't have gotten it back.

Goddamn club.

He stopped at the landing of the third floor.

This was where the fun began.

A cigarette girl blowing bubbles with a bright yellow plastic wand meandered toward him. A silver top hat was pinned at a jaunty angle on her head, her hair a tangle of blonde curls. She wore a white corseted dress with silver piping, and a silver sparkling bow tie attached to her slim neck. The skirt of her tight dress flared around the middle of her thighs with layers upon layers of ruffled tulle. Silver heels, similar to Lila's, were on the woman's feet, but it appeared she had no trouble walking on the metal grating.

She gestured to the black tray that hung from a thick black strap around the back of her neck and rested against her stomach. "Whaddya have?" she squawked in a Betty Boop voice.

Little vials of neon liquid filled the tray from edge to edge, holding anything from booze to drugs. He wasn't too keen on finding out.

When he shook his head, she blew bubbles into his face.

He reached to fan them away, but changed his mind and instead allowed one to rest on a fingertip. Curiously, it didn't pop on contact with his skin. He brought the iridescent sphere closer to his face.

A tiny black and orange butterfly hovering in the center, its wings lazily flapping in place.

He pushed the bubble into the air and it floated toward the vaulted ceiling.

"Whaddya have?" she asked again, pushing herself, and the tray, toward him.

"How did you do that?" he demanded.

"That's for me to know and for you to find out!" She ran off, laughing, dodging people in her path.

He quickly lost sight of her as she wove her way around the throng of partiers, some jostling him as they swallowed her. Not ten minutes into the club and his patience was already growing thin. He would look for his friends as he searched for a way out, and, well, if he found his way out first, his conscience would be okay with the fact that he'd tried.

He had no idea where to start, and he moved aimlessly through the crowd, women giving him the eye and brushing up along side him, arrogant men stepping on his feet, unwilling to move aside.

Music pounded, a creepy melody Ben recognized from The Birthday Massacre. Perfect atmosphere music.

"Hey, handsome."

A blonde woman wearing a champagne colored dress covered in sparkling sequins snagged the lapel of his jacket, pulling him toward her with surprising strength. She twirled them until she pressed him against the railing, pushed her body into his, and covered his lips with hers, burying her hands in his hair.

He stood there, hands hanging at his sides, too shocked to move, as she licked at him, her tongue tasting like bitter red wine.

Before he gathered his wits about him enough to push her away, she broke off the kiss. "Thanks, hon." She wiped her lips with the inside of her wrist, and blood trickled from the corner of her mouth.

She staggered, tripping over her high heels, and a gentleman in a tuxedo caught her, pulling her to him with a predatory look in his eyes aimed Ben's way.

Whatever the fuck she'd been drinking tasted like berries steeped in acid, and the metallic hint of blood in his mouth made bile rise in his throat.

Swallowing against the urge to throw up, he leaned against the rail, dancers gyrating below him, and he swirled saliva around his mouth with his tongue attempting to rinse the disgusting taste away. He wanted to spit, but instead he snagged a bottle of beer from a skinny Goth bartender manning a bar that must have been a mile long. Ben reached into his jacket to grab his wallet, but the bartender shook his head. "On the house," the he hollered over the music.

Ben nodded his thanks and brought the cold amber bottle to his lips. Everyone was giving him free booze tonight. He must look like he needed the drinks, but he hadn't thought of Megan since entering The Maze. No that wasn't true, he hadn't thought of her since meeting Lila. He was thinking about her instead, wondering where she and her group had ended up partying, or if the boys he'd seen going into the bar earlier partied with them.

Jealousy rolled in his gut.

Ben chose a hallway, any hallway. They shot off the center of the club like spokes of a bicycle wheel. He wouldn't find a door to the outside on the third floor, but possibly he could find a window or a fire escape. There needed to be fire exits to keep the building up to code.

Perspiration gathered beneath his arms and he flapped them uselessly. He was the only one wearing a jacket. Everyone else had dressed to the nines for an evening out on the town. All the diamonds and other jewels glinting in the strobing lights made him sick to his stomach when he knew a homeless man stood outside in the snow, his only source of warmth a fire in an old barrel.

Couples made out everywhere he turned. Sofas and settees, coffee tables and end tables littered the hallway he'd chosen. Strategically placed curtains and decorative screens created private alcoves, but this place was the last place he'd choose to make love. Tasteless and trashy. He couldn't wait to get out of there.

A tall brown-haired man shoved a red-headed woman against the black wall, and she dropped her drink. Liquid and glass splattered around their ankles but they didn't care —they didn't even notice. The man devoured her neck with his mouth, and the woman moaned in delight. He saw Ben watching and gave him a wolfish smile before going back to business.

Okay, not making love, as the woman laughed and grabbed for her partner's crotch, but he wasn't in the mood for a quick fuck, either.

Ben roamed the corridor; people strolled around drinking, kissing, talking. Closed door after door lined the black walls. Everywhere black besides the neon lights sparkling from the ceiling.

The whole place was disorientating, but it was supposed to be. The entire point of The Maze was to get lost. Figuratively, of course, with abundance of booze and drugs, but literally as well. It wasn't called The Maze for nothing, and from the accounts he'd heard from his friends, the bar lived up to its name.

The hallway didn't end—it went on forever. He could spend the entire evening searching this corridor alone, never mind the rest of the club, but he needed to start looking for whoever had called him asking for help. He paused to take a swig of beer, grateful the taste of blood on his tongue was gone.

He chose a door at random, turning the shining silver knob.

Cautiously, he opened the door.

Women dressed in their ballgowns and cocktail dresses sat at circular tables with their dates, men dressed in tuxedos and suits, much like the suit he wore under his jacket. Waiters weaved around the tables offering tea and coffee, replenishing . . . what seemed to be some kind of pastry, perhaps scones.

Tea time.

The room's walls were painted white and gold and glittered in the lights of the candles fastened to the walls in fancy sconces. Candles also decorated the tables that spotted the large room. Thin carpet covered the floor, cream with golden threads weaving floral patterns that complemented the walls.

No one noticed him.

Murmuring voices filled the room and Ben shut the

door not interested in joining a conversation or having tea. The beer in his hand was working for him perfectly fine.

He opened the door directly opposite the tea room. Inside, he discovered a movie viewing room. Waiters circled the room, offering to fill the audience's champagne flutes. They lounged in luxurious recliners.

Deborah Kerr sat beside Cary Grant in *An Affair to Remember*.

Leaning against the doorjamb, he got caught up for a moment, a sucker for an old movie.

Discouraged, he closed the door. At this rate he might as well sit somewhere and wait for the club to close. Finding whoever had called him would be a near impossible feat.

On the other hand, this would be the only time he would ever step foot inside The Maze, because God knew, he would never come back willingly. Maybe he should take advantage and explore. Megan had always called him a stick-in-the-mud, and he'd always objected. Preferring a simple, uncomplicated life did not make him boring. He liked quiet and comfortable.

With a resigned sigh, he opened the door next to the theatre and revealed a nail bar. A long row of pedicure chairs and foot tubs lined the black wall. At least twenty women sat getting their toes done by shirtless men kneeling at their feet, clad only in black dress pants and bow ties fastened around their necks, their pecs and abs gleaming in the overhead light.

Some of the women wiggled their fingers at him and Ben chuckled at the sight they made, their ballgowns gathered around their thighs.

Finding the scene strangely erotic, he shut the door.

This hallway offered activities for women, and he wanted to find a room that would interest him. A massage maybe, though he didn't need a happy ending, something he was sure The Maze would provide, or he could find some football on a TV somewhere. The Packers had played earlier in the evening, and he wanted to see the highlights or maybe a replay of the game.

Turing around, he gave up on that corridor and didn't bother to find the end. When he came back to the main area of the floor, he took a right away from the bar and the bartender who had given him the free beer.

Ben finished it and threw the bottle into the trash receptacle shaped like an octagon. He was walking away when the garbage can clattered and churned, and two gold coins clattered into a change slot positioned along the side.

Ben scooped them out and studied one. On one side a fairy flew, fluttering her golden wings.

He blinked. A trick of the light. It had to be. One beer wouldn't make him drunk.

He flipped the coin over. A huge tree grew from the bottom of the coin, leaves reaching the top. The leaves shimmered in an imaginary wind.

He dropped them into the pocket of his dress slacks.

What he wanted was to go home, but that wasn't going to happen anytime soon. He reached into his coat pocket for his phone to check the time. His hands dug around and found his wallet and keys but no phone.

The woman with the bloody mouth. She'd taken it when she body slammed him against the railing. Dammit. In the dark he never noticed her stumble off with it.

At least she hadn't taken his wallet. He'd need to keep the drinks coming. There was no way in hell he'd make it through this night sober. Not if he wanted to keep his sanity intact. This place was already driving him batshit crazy, and he hadn't even sampled a room yet.

He chose another hallway, and it was more of the same, black walls, black doors with silver knobs. More people kissing, drinking. He scoffed in disgust. Couldn't people do that at home? Why go to a club and do it in publ—oh. That was probably the whole point. He'd never felt the need for public displays of affection. He preferred being home, in the dark, perhaps a candle, maybe the glow of the TV playing *Casablanca*.

He pictured Lila sitting in one of the banquettes of The Lucky Clover. He wouldn't mind stealing a kiss or two in the shadows. Danny probably did it all the time. The lucky bastard.

Clinking the coins together in the pocket of his pants, he walked down the corridor, avoiding people stumbling into him as much as he could. Maybe the tokens were for purchasing drinks, or they were for condom machines in the restrooms. Ben huffed a laugh. There certainly seemed to be a need for that.

Ben ran a finger between his shirt collar and his neck. Christ was he hot.

A woman whispered in his ear from behind him. "You should have given Iris your jacket."

Ben whipped around and came face to face with a young Marilyn Monroe.

Impossible.

Yet here she was, wearing that famous white halter dress, her platinum hair coiffed perfectly in short wild curls around her head, her lips a bright crimson.

Marilyn held a diamond studded leash, a large orange Bengal tiger sitting patiently on the other end.

The big cat blinked his large brown eyes, and apprehensively, Ben leaned back. He'd never seen a tiger so close before, only in the zoos with bars or thick glass between them, but this cat seemed docile enough and he lowered to his haunches, intrigued. "Can I?"

Marilyn nodded. "Oh, sure."

Tentatively, Ben put a hand to the tiger's neck and to his delight, the tiger nuzzled his arm with his nose.

Marilyn giggled and patted the tiger on the head. Gently tugging the leash, she led the big cat through one of the black doors, and with his heart beating a mile a minute, he watched them go, the door closing firmly behind them.

He stood and tried the door, but it was locked and his hand fell away in disappointment.

Ben ambled along the hallway, curious to see how far he could go until he reached the end. Maybe he never would. Maybe it would lead to somewhere else, connect to a different hallway, or, pray to God, he would find an emergency exit.

Choosing a door at random, he easily turned a knob, and he slowly pushed it open.

The room contained an autumn wonderland.

A huge tree rained orange and brown leaves, the grass a bright green, the sky blue, dotted with puffy white clouds, but Ben barely saw any of it. A woman rested beneath the tree on a large handmade quilt, and a brown picnic hamper sat near her.

She was dressed like an extra from the HBO show *Game of Thrones*, complete with a white horse grazing near the tree, sniffing through the fallen leaves for choice grass.

The room drew him closer, into the tranquility that clashed harshly with the drunken excitement behind him.

"Shut the door."

Without hesitation, Ben did as he was told and to his disbelief the door dissolved, revealing nothing but rolling green hills for as far as his eyes could see.

VANIA RHEAULT

"Join me," the woman demanded, gesturing to an empty place on the quilt.

Ben walked across the floor carpeted with thick grass, though where he was couldn't be considered a room any longer.

The majestic horse whinnied, shaking his glimmering mane, the animal's coat shining in the bright sunlight. Its tail sparkled like strands of spider web, soft, light, translucent, blowing in the cool breeze that, unbelievably, caressed Ben's face.

"Would you care to sit?"

Ben silently obeyed the woman and sat in front of her, his legs crisscrossed as he had sat as a child in Kindergarten during story time.

"Are you hungry? It has been many hours since you've eaten." She opened the picnic basket and pulled out a delicate white plate, an intricate design of pink flowers painted in the center. She placed it in front of him.

Ben's stomach growled and his mouth watered when the woman placed a large sandwich on the plate, a grainy brown bread dripping with mayonnaise and mustard, fixings spilling from the middle: tomatoes, lettuce, and thick slices of meat.

He hadn't eaten since lunch, but sour thoughts of Megan had pushed his appetite away and he'd decided to go for a drink after work rather than eat dinner at home, alone.

"Go on," she encouraged, her voice a throaty purr.

Unable to resist, he picked up the sandwich and bit into it.

The woman withdrew a silver goblet from the basket and filled it with a red wine she poured from a black bottle.

Her wavy dark brown hair twisted around her shoulders in the light wind and a tiara, patterns of small flowers and leaves made with diamonds woven together in rose gold, rested upon her head. The neckline of her medieval white satin dress bared her shoulders, the corset pulling in her waist. She sat balanced on a hip, her bare feet peeking from beneath the hemline. When she raised her hand to take a sip of wine, the edge of her wide sleeve dripped to the ground.

She watched him eat, her eyes a golden amber. As fast as he was consuming the food, it made him self-conscious, but she only smiled and handed him a pewter tankard filled to the brim with cold water.

He downed the water gratefully, dehydrated from all the booze. The cool liquid traced a path down his throat, and he gasped for air after taking the last gulp from the mug.

She produced a white linen napkin, and Ben traded the mug for it. Only crumbs remained on the plate, and without a word, the woman returned it to the basket.

Satiated, the late hour hit him, but his eyelids snapped open when she spoke.

"You miss her."

Ben narrowed his eyes. "Who are you supposed to be, and how long have you worked here?"

Leaves still fell from the tree, and the horse still sniffed the sparkling green grass. Clouds drifted by, floating on a brilliant blue backdrop. It was all quite over-the-top, but he supposed it was what drew people in, time after time. As long as he was trapped, he would enjoy the ride.

"My name is Morgan le Fay." She paused. "Do you know who I am?"

Ben chuckled. This woman was a paid actress, much like the Marilyn look-a-like he'd met only moments ago. There was no way this could be her, *really* her, but Ben had always been a good sport and he'd play along. He shrugged. "King Arthur."

Morgan's smile lit her whole face. "Thank you. You have no idea how many people have not heard of me. I've tried many times to offer assistance, but I cannot if they do not know who I am."

This room didn't seem to have an obvious point, not like the nail bar, or the theatre, but at least he felt better after eating. He should have found a café or a restaurant in the club. In a place like this, there had to be somewhere to eat.

Ben was grateful for her kindness. He owed her a few minutes of conversation, at least, for feeding him. Though he wouldn't get far unless he found the door to the room, and as he considered the miles of rolling hills, that wouldn't be possible right now. He was a captive audience.

"If you want to help me, tell me about the phone call I received earlier. All I heard through the static was someone needing help and this address."

"This address?" she teased, throwing out her arms to encompass their surroundings.

"Well, no," Ben admitted. "For the club."

"I . . . see," Morgan said, though it was clear she didn't.

"The Maze."

"I know of no maze, but the one to your heart. Many have tried and failed to reach it."

"Megan had it," Ben blurted, caught off guard by the change of subject.

Morgan reached across the quilt and rested her hand on his. Her fingers glinted with several gold rings, and a massive emerald in a band of gold encircled her ring finger. Her thumb rubbed against his knuckles, now white from the pressure of his clenched fist.

"Then why did she go?"

Defeated, Ben lay on his side, propped up by his elbow. The autumn breeze cooled him, but he wished he could take off his jacket. He was afraid of losing it now, and he wouldn't want to be outside without it.

"I don't know."

Morgan shook her head. "Yes, you do. Do not do yourself such a disservice by denying what you know to be true."

"I treated her like a queen," Ben disagreed angrily. "I bought her a house, gave her a cat. I gave her everything she wanted. She chose her own engagement ring, which she kept."

"I am a queen as well," Morgan reminded him.

Her history came back to him, though he hadn't read her story in many years. Morgan le Fay, wed to King Urien, but forever in love with Sir Lancelot, one of the Knights of the Round Table.

Sympathy brimmed in her eyes. "You speak of the material things you gave to her, yet no mention of love. Ben, you did not love her."

He knew he didn't, hadn't, but they had been good friends, affectionate. So what if his heart hadn't pounded when he was around her, so what if she hadn't made him sweat like he was now in his goddamn wool jacket, but they had never argued. They had agreed on everything, even the number of children they would have.

"There was no passion. You cannot ask a woman to love, to live, without passion."

Ben remembered the heat in his belly when his eyes had met Lila's, how her touch had made him hard even though he'd only known her for a few moments.

He'd been wrong to ask Megan to live without passion, and he'd been wrong to ask it of himself.

As soon as he was free of The Maze, he would find the woman of his dreams and truly fall in love with her.

As soon as he forgot Lila's smile.

A gust of wind blew, twirling the fallen leaves around the brown tree trunk, and with it, blowing away Ben's remaining resentment over Megan's betrayal. He should be thanking her for seeing what he hadn't wanted to see, and for the first time since she left him, he was happy she found someone else. He may not be pleased with the way she had gone about it, but she'd had the courage to do something before it was too late.

"Your mind and heart are at ease," Morgan commented, reaching into the basket and pulling out a plate of chocolate cake and a small dessert fork. "Eat. You will need your strength."

His mouth watered at the sight of the thick piece of cake. Since he was a boy, chocolate had always been his favorite, and he wouldn't doubt that somehow Morgan knew that. Sweating under his jacket, he wished he had more water and just then she handed him a goblet of red wine.

"You don't know what happened to my friends?" Ben asked. He hadn't recognized the voice on the line. It could have been any one of his friends, but it also could have been a wrong number. Chances of him finding out were slim to none. Not in a place like this.

"The Maze is full of joy, but it is also full of pain. You must beware, Ben. You must find your way out."

"If I wait until the club closes—"

"No!"

Her sharp objection startled him, and he sloshed wine over the rim, staining the white quilt. The liquid soaked into the material.

"The Maze never closes. If you do not find your way out, it will never let you go."

The look in Morgan's golden eyes made him bite back any protest. "All right."

Morgan waited patiently as he downed the last of the wine and finished his cake. She placed the plate and both their goblets into the basket.

"Morgan, I wish . . ." Ben stopped.

Morgan le Fay was a fictional character; her unhappiness was a lesson, not a situation he could fix for her.

She stood, a faint smile touching her lips. "I appreciate the sentiment," she said wryly, "but perhaps you should be thinking of your own predicament."

A kind way of telling him to mind his own business. He laughed, standing as well.

"Help me up," she asked, and Ben helped her mount the white horse, lacing his fingers together as a foothold.

Morgan hoisted herself onto the stallion's back and sat astride, smoothing the horse with long firm strokes along its neck.

"Thank you," Ben said.

She looked a fine Queen sitting atop her horse, her tiara glinting in the sun, her hair streaming down her back in thick waves. "You are a good man, Ben. Good luck to you."

Before he could reply, she nudged the horse forward, and the horse bolted across the vibrant green grass. Morgan's hair trailed behind her, the skirt of her dress flapping against the horse's flanks.

The moment she was out of sight, the sky, grass, and tree fell away, and Ben stood in the busy hallway of the club, people pushing past him, music pounding in his ears.

He tried to find his bearings. That hadn't been a dream. He felt full, the taste of chocolate and wine still on his lips.

Ben abandoned the hallway and searched for another. He passed by several before choosing one. This was a lot like Russian Roulette; he could live to see another day or get shot with a bullet right between the eyes.

He didn't want to venture too deep into the new hallway, and he chose a door at its mouth, on his immediate right.

He twisted the silver doorknob on the black door and stepped inside the dark room. The door swung shut behind him with a deafening snap and he clawed at the door in a panic, shaking the doorknob trying to free himself.

He almost went into cardiac arrest when the word "Stop" slithered through the blackness and down his spine; gooseflesh crawled over his skin. He took a deep breath and searched for the source of the voice, though his vision had not yet adapted to the lack of light.

A single flame flickered to life in the middle of the room, and an older woman stood holding the candle near her face, her purple eyes narrowed as she stared at him. Her hair, shot with fine strands of silver, was pinned behind her head and her cheekbones stood out prominently, a milky white. Violet lipstick graced her full lips which were stretched into a mocking smile.

She wore a black velvet dress, a black cape resting on her shoulders and flowing down her body to pool at her feet. Her dress's neckline plunged and several heavy strands of silver hung from her neck.

Another room with special effects. Perhaps the cover for the club had actually been as much as the fifty he'd given The Maze's hostess. These actresses didn't come cheap.

The light gradually grew brighter, and to his right, two glass caskets were displayed on golden pedestals. A woman, dressed in rags, her beautiful golden hair tied back in a kerchief, kneeled on her hands and knees scrubbing the floor near them, her scrub brush rasping against the stone.

Farther across the room loomed a huge tower, and a woman leaned out the small window, her hair, as bright as a yellow dandelion, fell to the ground in thick cascading waves.

An ocean crashed against a shore in the distance.

"Who are you?"

"Many call me the Evil Queen," she replied, her voice hard.

Ben blinked. That could have made her anyone at all. "Are you from a book?"

The Evil Queen shrugged. "Does it matter?"

"I don't suppose it does," Ben agreed easily, stepping over to one of the caskets.

A woman with blonde wavy hair and pink lips lay sleeping inside, her dainty hands folded under her breasts which gently rose and fell with each shallow breath. She wore a teal dress, the bodice tied with a white ribbon.

She was too beautiful to be real.

"Sleeping Beauty?" he asked, taken aback.

"Yes."

Ben peered inside the other casket. This glass box contained a woman with rich black hair, cherry red lips, wearing a yellow dress. She was younger than Sleeping Beauty.

The Evil Queen stood next to Ben, her hand on his shoulder.

"Snow White, I'm guessing?" Ben asked.

"Indeed."

Ben had no interest in fairy tales. He'd known Morgan because he liked knights and had read King Arthur in school. "What do you want with me? Let me out."

The Evil Queen threw her head back and laughed. "Oh, if I had a gold coin for every time someone begged that of me, I would be very rich."

A trickle of unease tightened in his gut. She was a real, living, breathing person, and he was trapped in a room with her. Not as friendly as Morgan, the Evil Queen wouldn't be offering him wine and cake. "What are you doing with them?" he asked.

The Evil Queen traced a finger over the gold piping of the glass coffin that protected Snow White during her slumber. "I watch over them."

"That doesn't make any sense." The words slipped out of his mouth but it was too late to take them back.

The Evil Queen stabbed him with a glare and grabbed his chin, her fingernails puncturing the skin covering his jaw. "It makes every bit of sense, you fool."

"Explain it to me then," Ben murmured, hoping to calm her.

There was an insanity in her eyes, a despair, and he was afraid if he pissed her off she would do something particularly unpleasant to him. They were all alone and no one was looking for him. If he disappeared, there would be none the wiser, at least until Monday when he didn't show up for work.

"The princesses, Sleeping Beauty and Snow White. Why are they here? Their princes came for them and rescued them."

The woman scrubbing the floor choked out a bitter laugh.

Ben jerked his face from the Evil Queen's grasp, her nails scratching a path over his jaw. He recognized the woman, her blue dress in tatters, her hands red and chapped from scrubbing.

"Cinderella?"

She fully faced him and he winced. A large, deep purple bruise covered the side of her face that had been hidden in shadows. Someone had hit her not long ago, and they had not held back.

He rushed to her, knelt on the damp soapy stone, and gently cupped her face in his hands. "Why are you here, love?" he asked. Her faded blue eyes leaked tears and pain and her lips trembled.

"My prince did not come for me."

Ben remembered the fairy tale. He had never watched a movie version, but the plot was well-known and he didn't need to see the end to know the prince found her after the whole glass slipper thing.

"What do you mean? You went to the ball . . ."

Cinderella nodded, tears dripping off her chin. "I went to the ball, I ran away, and I had to leave my slipper behind. I was so very much in a hurry," she whispered.

Her voice mesmerized him. He wanted to rescue her himself. "And the prince, Prince Charming, he searched his kingdom looking for you."

"He searched," Cinderella agreed, resuming her scrubbing, her knuckles cracked and bleeding. "But he did not find me, and he gave up. Stepmother had hidden me away so very well, you see."

Ben fell backward, his hands catching his fall. "What do you mean, he gave up?"

He staggered to his feet, meeting the Evil Queen's eyes with disbelief. That wasn't the way the story went, how the story ended. Cinderella was supposed to have been rescued, was supposed to have been taken to the castle and married to her Prince and lived happily ever after.

"What about Sleeping Beauty?" He rested his hands

against the coffin, peering through his own reflection to the sleeping princess inside.

"You know the story?"

"Not well." It had been many years since hearing the tale, and there were so many versions.

"An evil fairy placed a curse on Sleeping Beauty on the day of her birth. On her sixteenth birthday she would prick her finger on a spinning wheel and die."

Ben nodded; he *did* know this part.

"A good fairy was able to slightly alter the curse and instead of dying, Sleeping Beauty fell into a deep sleep. The good fairy and her sisters placed a spell on the city and all the castle's inhabitants, including Sleeping Beauty's parents, the King and Queen. The fairies protected the city and castle with a multitude of trees and thorns, creating a protective barrier against anyone who would try to harm the city's citizens or the royal family. A hundred years passed.

"A journeying prince was told the story during his travels, and he went to investigate. When he saw the barrier, he gave up and moved on."

"Rapunzel."

The woman leaned from the window, keening as if her heart was broken, never to be repaired.

The Evil Queen nodded. "The prince who found her was no match for the woman who had stolen her. One day he visited the tower, and he was tricked by the woman. Through his own weakness he allowed her to overpower him, and he was thrown from the tower to his death. Now Rapunzel is trapped in the tower forever."

"How many princesses do you have here?"

There were the coffins, the tower, and in the distance, the walls faded into a patchwork of greys and blues. He took a step toward it, having always been enthralled with the sea.

The Evil Queen nodded her acquiescence, and Ben walked across the room as it faded and seeped into the shore of a beach, the ocean churning with storm. Seagulls spread their wings against the sky dark with clouds. A cool wet wind blew from the water, misting Ben's face.

The waves licked at the toes of Ben's shoes, sea foam reaching for his foot like little fingers.

There was only one fairy tale Ben knew of that had anything to do with the ocean. *The Little Mermaid*. He thought of the most popular version with the singing crab, the talking seagull, and Ben knew without asking this tale would not lead to a happily ever after for the mermaid, either. "She trades her voice for human legs."

"Yes," the Evil Queen agreed. "But even for all the time she spends with the prince, he marries another. The mermaid is offered the chance to return to the ocean to live out her days if she kills the prince, and she finds him in his wedding bed with his princess. But the mermaid does not have the heart to take his life, for she loves him still, and she flings herself into the water, turning to sea foam for her failure."

Ben bent down and ran his fingertips along the bubbles caressing the shore. "She's here?"

"I protect her as I do the others."

"Why?"

The Evil Queen shrugged and linked her arm with his. The candle disappeared from her hand, and it sat now, on a large wooden table. An enormous mirror attached to a golden stand stood nearby, and the candle's flickering fire reflected in the glass.

"Because men are fools. If they had done what they were supposed to do, if they had done what was right, none of these women would be here, living out their lives in misery, in heartache. If those men had been but strong enough."

Ben pulled away from her. Her eyes had caught fire, her cheeks rosy from rage. He didn't lie to himself; he was frightened of her. "What do you want from me?"

"I want you to do what you are supposed to do. You let her slip from your fingers; you walked away from her. She needs you, yet you think nothing of abandoning her in her time of need. How will she survive if you do not do your part?" She backed him across the floor.

Ben was desperate to keep space between them.

"Are you talking about Meg—"

No, he hadn't walked away from Megan. He'd walked away from Lila. He'd given her a brief look before stepping out of The Lucky Clover into the cold night's air.

"Lila belongs to someone else."

"You stupid fool," the Evil Queen howled.

A sliver of a story came back to him. "You're the Evil Queen. You're Snow White's stepmother. You tried to kill her with a poisonous apple."

"Indeed," the Evil Queen purred. "But what the prince did to her was a million times worse than anything I ever did." She traced a long, dark purple fingernail down his cheek.

Ben flinched, his skin raw from her earlier attack. "What the prince did? He didn't kiss her and wake her up?"

"Of course not, or she would not be here. The prince saw her lying in her glass coffin, made by her stupid little dwarf friends, took in her beauty, and decided there was no way to save her. He abandoned her, as the rest."

Ben stumbled into the Evil Queen's mirror. He shouldn't have asked; he shouldn't have provoked her.

The Evil Queen grabbed the lapels of his jacket,

bringing her face centimeters away from his. "Stop being such a fool and find her."

"I don't know where to look," Ben protested, hypnotized by her violet eyes framed with long dark lashes. The mirror hadn't lied; she was one of the most beautiful women he had ever seen.

She licked her lips. "Then let me help you."

The Evil Queen pushed him into the mirror, and he fell.

CHAPTER THREE

Ben barely caught his breath before a door opened and he was dragged inside another room.

"Get down!" someone yelled, pushing on his shoulder.

He was shoved to the ground, and he leaned against a tree trunk, the damp grass wetting his pants.

This room was dark as well, and Ben blinked rapidly to orientate himself to the new atmosphere. The popping sounds in the distance grated on his nerves after spending time with the Evil Queen in her quiet room.

"Here, this will calm ya down."

A flask landed in his lap, and he unscrewed the top. He smelled the contents and took a gulp. Whiskey burned his throat and made a hot path to his gut. "What's going on?"

"We gotta save the girl."

For fuck's sake. He didn't want to play a game. He wanted to find his friends and a way out. He wanted to see Lila, though that would have to wait until tomorrow, or, ah, later today. Desire mixed with the whiskey. And not for sex. Well, not *only* for sex. Companionship. Friendship. A contentment found only when finally finding the right person to spend the rest of his life with.

Impatiently, he looked around this room. He'd been pulled into some kind of forest. Nighttime, a mist floated through the treetops.

"Where are we?"

This room beat all the others by far. He would swear on a stack of Bibles that they were really outside. The air was crisp and clean, with just a small amount of woodsmoke to heighten his senses and make him believe a bonfire was burning somewhere not too far into the distance.

The man next to him was dressed in black jeans, a black skin-tight Henley shirt, and he was hugging a rifle close to his chest. A black backpack was strapped to his back. He was shivering with cold. Or maybe excitement. It was hard to tell.

"The woods, dipshit. Can't you see that?" He slanted Ben a glance through narrowed eyes. "You got a piece on ya by chance?"

"No!"

"Too bad. But you still have your coat. Smart bastard. It's fucking cold out here. You're lucky you didn't check when you got here." He cocked his rifle. "Come on."

"Where are we going? What kind of room is this?"

"They have the girl, and we need to save her. You ever play Flag in school? Name's Cy."

"Ben. Flag? Yeah, sure."

On his hands and knees he followed Cy, crawling from the security of the tree trunk. He still gripped the flask, and he wasn't going to give it back. With the way his night was going, he was going to need it. He slipped it into the pocket of his jacket. Cy was right. It was colder than hell out here. Well, everywhere was colder than hell, but whatever.

Ben had been forced to play Flag at summer camp. They'd been split into two groups, pitted against each other, a white flag at stake. The first group to reach it, defend it, and take out the other group won the game. He'd always come home covered in bites and scratches, his eyes watering from the gnats flying into his face, sunburn crackling his skin.

"We're going after a *flag?*" he furiously whispered. *Goddamn it* for getting sucked into something like this.

"No. Haven't you been listening? We need to rescue the girl."

"What girl?"

"The girl those sumbitches kidnapped. We gotta get to her."

A snapping twig cut off their conversation, and a huge muscled man dressed in camo fatigues approached, his rifle trained on them.

Cy quickly lifted his gun.

Ben reared back at the sound of the gunshot, his throat working in stunned disbelief as the man stumbled and fell to the ground, a bright red spot blooming on his chest.

"What the f-fuck was that?" Ben stuttered. He had never seen anyone shot in real life, only in movies and the war documentaries his father liked to watch.

"You wanted to get shot?" Cy asked. "He wasn't fucking around. Just saved your life, pal. Listen, bad guys in camo, good guys in black. All you need to know."

"Hey!" he grabbed Cy's shoulder. "What the fuck? These guns are real? Not toys? Jesus Christ."

"What the fuck do you think we're playing?" Cy huffed, his breath coming out in white puffs in the frozen air. "We gotta get out of here. The girl is through those trees a ways. The Camos got to her first. We hafta find other members of

Team Black so we have backup. I wish to hell you had a piece."

"Wouldn't matter. I'm not shooting anybody."

Cy shook his head. "Come on."

They made their way across the forest floor, darting from tree to tree, Cy vibrating with nervous energy.

"How many of you guys are out here?"

Cy sucked in a lungful of air through his nose. They were leaning against another tree trunk. The night was cold, the stars, those he saw through the dense tree line, sparkled white against the pure black sky.

"The Camo group is motherfucking huge." Cy laughed. "Well, not anymore. Been pickin' them off like flies." He kissed his rifle. "Us? I don't know how many of us are left."

He followed Cy through the woods as quietly as he could, as to not attract attention. He was relieved to be dressed in black; it made things easier. "What are the Camos going to do with the girl?"

The whole thing sounded farfetched to him, but Cy seemed more than serious, and that Camo guy that Cy shot hadn't moved one inch after he fell to the ground. And holy shit, all that blood looked real.

"Only God knows," Cy muttered ominously.

Ben didn't question how Cy knew where they were going, but Cy moved through the woods with ease, holding the rifle as if he had all his life. "You a hunter?" he whispered.

"I've been known to take down a deer or two with my dad," Cy nodded, though Ben could barely see it. "Hold up."

Cy stopped him as he was about to step from their hiding position behind a large tree trunk. "Look," Cy hissed, tilting his chin.

A campfire glowed through a scattering of trees. Three Camos were sitting around it, trying to get warm, and a member of Team Black sat off to the side, his hands bound behind his back, a swath of black cloth tied around his mouth, gagging him.

"They've got one of ours."

Ben balked at being included, but he would be considered part of Team Black if anyone saw him dressed how he was, and there wasn't anything he could do about it.

He pressed against the tree and took a chance to peer around the huge trunk, taking another look at the bound man. He looked familiar. Yeah. "Fuck."

"What? Don't tell me you're scared to take those mofos out. Three against two, maybe three, if we can get our guy loose."

"No, that's not it."

Though Ben hadn't been in a fight since grade school when he'd been defending his milk money on the playground, he felt calm approaching the Camos. This was a game of Flag. He was still in The Maze. There wasn't anything illegal going on.

Cy had shot an actor, that's all. The ultimate role playing game.

As soon as the game was over, they would be free to go.

He hoped.

"Then what is it?"

"That guy of ours" —Ben winced as he included himself— "he looks like a friend of mine. Simon?"

"You're Ben!" Cy exclaimed. "Fuck me over twice with a baseball bat. I didn't make the connection. A while back he was trying to get a hold of you, before we got separated."

"I got phone call. I didn't hear much except the address

to The Maze. I didn't, I mean, I *don't*, know what's going on."

Cy clapped him on the shoulder and squeezed, meeting his eyes. "No one does, brother, no one does. Let's save his ass!" Cy bounded from tree to tree, expertly keeping cover, his gun close to his chest.

Jesus Christ. It had to be two in the morning, if not later, he was stuck in some game he hadn't played for twenty years, and he desperately needed a drink. He took a deep lungful of cold air. He didn't dare, though he fingered the flask he hadn't returned to Cy. He might quite possibly be the only sane person around.

Cy jerked the butt of the rifle. Cy wanted him to follow. Now. He was crouching and making his way toward the fire before Ben could stop him.

A movement caught his eye and out of the shadows came another Camo. Cy didn't see him in time to react, and Camo slammed him on the temple with the butt of his rifle.

With a weak cry, Cy fell to the ground.

"Hey," Ben burst out, stepping from behind the tree. "That wasn't necessary. This is a fucking game." Keeping an eye on Camo, he helped Cy to his feet.

Cy might be blockhead, but he didn't deserve that.

"Hmmmph!"

"Shut the hell up!" One of the Camos who had been sitting around the campfire kicked Simon in the ribs and he howled through his gag.

"Looks like we got ourselves a couple of prisoners," one of the other Camos commented from where he sat by the fire.

"Are you all right?" Ben asked Cy.

Cy's temple was bleeding, but he nodded.

"Who does shit like that?" Ben glared at the Camo who hit Cy. "Come on."

He nudged Cy toward the fire.

Cy reluctantly followed. "We should listen to these guys," he whispered.

"No! I'm done playing this game. I want to go back to the club and get a drink." He knelt by Simon who was panting, tears running down his face. "Hey buddy."

Ben helped his friend sit up, untied the piece of black material, and pulled it from Simon's mouth.

"Ben! Thank Jesus. Where the hell have you been?"

Ben untied Simon's hands. Luckily he wasn't bound with anything that needed a knife. While Ben had been a Boy Scout, he wasn't prepared for something like this.

"Where the hell have *I* been? Are you fucking kidding me? You're lucky I'm here at all. Do you know what I've gone through since I got to the club? How in the hell did you expect me to find you?"

Simon rubbed his eyes, righted his wire-rimmed glasses, and shook out his hands to get the circulation back.

"Both of you, to your feet, now!"

"Hey. It's a game, chill out. It's a goddamn flag." Fatigue was catching up with him, and his temper flared.

"No, they have a woman," Simon corrected him. "The winning team keeps her."

"And that's us. Can't wait to get a piece of that," one of the Camos growled appreciatively, rubbing his hands together.

It was true then. Before the night was done, he was going to have to help Simon and Cy rescue this woman. If she'd been pulled into this game as he had, she was an innocent pawn, and it wouldn't be like him not to try his best to help.

"You alone?" Ben asked Simon under his breath.

"Alan and Kip were with me. I don't know where they are now. Felix came to the club with us, but I don't think he's here in the woods," Simon said.

"We gotta get this woman and get out of here. Out of the club. How did you get sucked in here?"

Before Simon could answer, Ben felt a jab in his lower back. Instinctively, he raised his arms above his head in surrender.

"Let's get moving. I'm tired of all the bullshit. Move out."

Now it was four against three, with an extra Camo who'd come out of nowhere.

Ben met Cy's and Simon's eyes in an effort to keep them cool. They were overpowered and outmanned. If they were going to win, they needed to be smart about this.

They walked through the woods, the cold biting into Ben's face. His fingertips tingled. He didn't dare think how Cy and Simon were holding up with only their clubbing clothes.

"I'm sorry about Megan," Simon offered, stumbling over the forest floor. He'd never been one for being outside, and it showed, tripping over the smallest stick.

"Megan?" Cy asked curiously.

Simon nodded. "Megan was Ben's fiancée. She left him for another guy."

"That's rough," Cy said.

"Yeah," Simon agreed. "She was sweet too, and the best baker. God, the cakes she would make. Ben invited us over to watch the Packers play, and she made this cheesecake. It tasted better than sex. Take the best sex you've ever had and times it by a thousand. That's how good it was."

Cy grunted. "I don't know. If I did that with the best sex

I ever had, I think I'd end up with a cupcake, no, maybe a muffin. Bran."

"Oh, no, no. No. That's no good at all," Simon replied earnestly. "Listen, when we get out of here my sister has a friend—"

"Do you mind?" Ben asked sharply.

"Hey, just because you haven't had any since Megan left, you don't have to take it out on us." Simon shot him an injured look.

He felt like a piece of shit for making Simon feel bad after getting kicked in the ribs. "Sorry," he muttered.

"No problem." Simon gave him a puppy dog grin. "I really am sorry about Megan."

"Can I have your sister's friend's number?" one of the Camos asked.

Camo's friend slapped him alongside the back of his head. "Shut the fuck up."

Ben continued to sidestep over fallen branches and bracken. Metal glinted in the moonlight and he paused to kick it. It was solid. Camo didn't allow him to investigate further and pushed him over the thick metal strip.

"Where are we going?" Ben felt the sharp poke of the rifle through his jacket.

The Camos ignored him, but Cy responded. "They have base not much farther from here."

Base. Ben wanted to laugh. He felt ten, playing cowboys and Indians, with home base belonging to the neighbor kid next door. They'd had a strong enough tree for a treehouse, something Ben had envied for months. "Is that where Kip and Alan are?"

"I have no idea."

It wasn't long before Camo pushed him into a clearing. A huge bonfire was burning in the center, and men dressed in grey-green camouflage sat around it, some sitting on large rocks, some on the ground, two on a fallen tree trunk.

Members of Team Black sat on the ground in a circle, their backs pressed against each other. The Camos ignored them, talking among themselves, shivering.

Ben, Cy, and Simon were pushed none too gently near the others, and he spotted Kip and Alan. They were staring at a phone, oblivious to everything around them. Apparently the situation wasn't as grave as it appeared to be, if his friends were watching—

"Hey," he whispered to them, bending down, Simon at his back. Cy was high-fiving some of his team, reunited after a long night of, ah, killing.

"Ben, you made it!" Alan exclaimed, keeping one eye on the phone.

"Ben, this shit's intense!"

Ben assumed Kip was talking about the situation, the Camos waiting for them to try to escape. "I know. We need a plan to get out of here. I've put up with this shit long enough."

"No, no, not that," Kip said, pulling on Ben's sleeve like a little kid. "This." Kip shoved the phone into Ben's face.

"You're watching porn? At a time like this? And how the hell are you getting signal out here in the middle of no where?" Ben was furious. When had his friends become such sex fiends?

"Hey, what else are we supposed to do? They got guns. We don't. We went to The Maze to do a little gambling. No harm done. Then we chose the wrong door and got sucked into some weird-ass *Lord of the Flies* bullshit," Alan said, waving his hands.

"Simon said Felix was with you."

"We lost him back at the club."

That was something anyway. He didn't want to keep track of any more of his friends. "So what's this about some girl?" He eyed the Camos guarding them. They didn't seem to be taking this seriously at all, standing around talking, their guns hanging at their sides. At least they weren't watching porn.

Kip shut his phone off and shoved it into his pocket. "She's over there, sitting with the leader of the other team." He lowered his voice. "Ben, I don't know what the fuck this is, but I think people are dying out there, like, man, this isn't just a game."

Shifting on his haunches, Ben nodded. "I agree. We need a distraction, or a diversion. These fuckers aren't messing around, and we can't leave this girl sitting here as a prize. She has a family or something."

"Thanks for the concern guys." Simon knelt near Ben in front of Kip and Alan and gave his friends the finger.

"We knew you could handle it, buddy. Listen, after we get out of this, it would be great if you could fix me up with Heidi—"

"Hey, if that's his sister's friend, I get dibs first. I got bran muffins over here," Cy interrupted.

"What the fuck is he talking about?" Kip asked.

"Nothing. Cy, we need a distraction. I think we stand a good chance of getting out of here."

If Ben didn't get control of the situation he was going to explode. Usually his friends gave him good comic relief; they had been a big help in the immediate days after Megan left him. Going out, when he felt like it, was always a blast. There was never a dull moment with Simon, Kip, and Alan.

And Felix. Felix had been a rock. Ben wasn't sure if he would ever be able to repay the man.

His friends were a good group of guys.

"Yeah, I think I got something."

They spoke in whispers, and over the crackling fire it didn't seem as if the Camos heard them. They didn't appear concerned. If they were bored, cold, and resentful, it could be to their advantage.

Cy joined them and they formed a group within the group. He took off his backpack and unzipped it. "What were you thinking?"

"I don't want to hurt anyone," Ben said immediately, "and I want to rescue the girl. Get her back to The Maze. She probably wasn't alone and her friends, or boyfriend, husband, whatever, they're probably worried about her."

Cy dug in his backpack. "Here. Hold these. I don't want them going off."

Ben held out his hands and swore under his breath. Cy shoved two very real-looking hand grenades at him, and he had a feeling these were not toys. "What the hell are these?"

Innocence plastered all over his face, Cy said, "Standard issue."

"Christ. We aren't using these."

"I know. They're not what I was digging for. Here. These are the ticket, and I have a ton of the bastards." Cy began handing out little black cylinders.

"I'm afraid to ask." And he was. Cy could have anything in that backpack.

"Smoke bombs, yes!" This came from Simon who was excitedly unscrewing the top.

"How do you know?" Ben asked, irritated. He wasn't quite sure smoke bombs were the way to go, either. They seemed harmless enough, but would they do the job?

"I bought some on Amazon, you know, for the thing," Simon said, blinking.

Ben didn't remember what thing, but Simon talked like

he'd been there. He would ask later, but for right now, he couldn't waste the time to care. He wanted to get this going.

Cy passed the smoke bombs along to the group, and the Camos watched them, but no one came over to investigate.

Ben was relieved. He didn't want them tipped off. The element of surprise would be their only defense against a group so heavily armed.

The bomb Simon released began to stream smoke.

"What the fuck are you doing?" one of the Camos demanded as a light grey smoke clouded the group.

It was now or never, but Cy was one step ahead of him. With a screech, Cy kicked out at a Camo's knee and the man fell to the ground, dropping his rifle.

The next few minutes were utter pandemonium and Ben lost track of who was doing what to whom as the guys on Team Black threw their smoke bombs into the clearing. In seconds, thick grey smoke filled the entire clearing.

Before it grew too heavy, on his belly, he slithered in the general direction of the girl. He hadn't seen her, even after Kip pointed in her direction.

It didn't take long before he found her alone near the campfire, sitting on the ground. The leader of the Camos had abandoned her to help his teammates. Leaving the flag alone was the one thing you did not do. The stupid fools would rather fight than win.

Good.

Smoke clouded the area, the bitter smell stinging his nose and making his eyes water.

When he got his first clear look at her, his heart sank. Her eyes were covered with a blindfold, her arms bound behind her. Even over the din she must have heard him approach, and she tilted her head.

"Who's there? What's happening?"

Her hair was still pinned at the back of her head, some strands coming loose, framing her face, trailing down her back. Her green dress was stained with dirt. Somewhere along the way she had lost her silver sandals. The Camos might have made her take them off so she could move faster through the woods.

"I'm going to get you out of here . . . Lila." Ben brushed the back of her head to remove the blindfold but found the knot was too tight. He started on the binding at her wrists instead. The knot felt looser, and he worked at it with cold fingertips.

"You know who I am? Are you playing the game?"

Ben chuckled, freeing her arms. "No."

She let out a cry as her arms fell to her sides and the circulation returned to her hands.

"Shh. It's okay. I know you must be freezing." Ben rubbed her arms for a moment, warming her skin and helping the circulation come back to her arms. He took off his jacket and wrapped it around her. He felt as if they were in a bubble, a cocoon, just the two of them, disguised by the smoke. He hadn't been entirely sure he would ever see her again, and now here he was, draping his jacket over her shoulders, hugging her to warm her.

The sounds of the fight drifted away. He no longer heard the banshee cries of the men, the erratic gunshots.

He cradled her against his chest. "I want to get you away from here, but you have to trust me, okay? I'll take off your blindfold when we have more time. I don't want to get caught."

"You sound familiar."

The waver in her voice broke his heart. He hoped she hadn't been out here long. It was so cold, and she was wearing her little dress and nothing more. She might have died of hypothermia or been on her way to it. "Are you okay? How are you feeling? Are you cold?"

"I'm hungry," she admitted. "Thirsty. I had a blanket until not long ago. I don't know what they did with it."

"At least that was something," he muttered, standing, one arm behind her back, the other arm under her legs.

Her head fit perfectly into the curve of his shoulder.

It was surprisingly easy to walk away from the fight without being detected.

Ben walked with her for a long while, putting as much space between them and the fight as he could, not daring to stop in case the Camos realized their prize was gone. He hoped his friends and the rest of Team Black fared well. He would hear the story at some point. No one would actually get stuck in The Maze, despite what Morgan told him. It was a dance club, nothing more.

He found a small grass clearing and sat with her in his lap. They hadn't spoken, he being so intent on escaping and listening for anyone following them, but he didn't know what they would talk about anyway. He'd rescued her, sure, but he didn't know her. He didn't know if she would have remembered him well enough to pick him out of a lineup a week from now.

"Who are you? Why did you save me? Don't you want to win the game?"

Ben secured the jacket around her and started working on the blindfold, careful not to pull her hair. "I did. I have the prize, don't I?"

She laughed as he pulled the blindfold away from her eyes, but her laughter died as their gazes met. "Ben."

She burrowed her face into his chest, and he took that as an invitation to pull her closer. "How in the hell did you get out here?" He spoke gruffly, out of concern. "Where are all your friends?"

Lila spoke into his shirt. "When we got to The Maze, we were separated almost right away. I had to go to the bathroom, and the others went to get drinks and dance. After I was done in the bathroom, a guy in a tux—I thought he worked at the club—told me he would help me find my friends. Instead, he led me down a hallway and pushed me through a door, and, I don't know how, but I fell into the woods. Before I could look for help to get back to the club I was taken hostage in the game. It could have been worse, I guess."

Her voice had faded as she told her tale. Ben believed her. With what he'd experienced tonight, Lila was lucky this was all that had happened to her. Still, it was enough.

"Getting warmer?" he asked.

"Yeah. I'm lucky you didn't check your jacket. Thanks."

"I didn't plan on being in The Maze for long. I got a call from someone saying they needed my help and this address. I've never been here before, and I'll never come back here again."

Lila laughed, and he tightened his arms around her, until he remembered she wasn't his.

"Lila, where's Danny? Shouldn't you have called him for help?"

"I left my phone in my jacket. My dress doesn't have pockets, and I hate shoving it in my bra."

"Won't he be worried you haven't gotten home yet? My phone was stolen, or I would check the time and call him for you."

Lila clutched his jacket to her. "We don't live together. He won't know what time I get back."

Ben didn't know what to do with that. He wanted it to

59

mean she and Danny weren't close, maybe not even a couple, but he remembered the love and affection in Danny's eyes when he looked at her and he knew it wasn't true. Her living arrangements with her boyfriend weren't any of his business, but that wouldn't stop him from finding out.

"We should probably keep moving. We need to find a way back." He ran a hand up and down her leg. Her skin was cold, and her feet felt like blocks of ice. She wore pantyhose, or tights, but they wouldn't do much to keep her warm.

Sounding forlorn Lila said, "It seems impossible," and her breath came out in white puffs.

"Have you ever been to The Maze before?" he asked, folding around her to keep her warm.

"No. Brigid wanted to try it. I didn't want to, I thought we were going to other bars downtown. I changed my mind after we went in though. The hallways and doors, the dance floor, the levels. It was all so spectacular. Even going to the bathroom was amazing. I just wanted to pee, but there was a spa inside. You could stay for any kind of treatment: facial, massage, a woman was even getting her hair cut. It was baffling and marvelous all at the same time."

Ben remembered the Evil Queen and he shook his head. "The Maze isn't all fun and games. I watched Cy shoot someone and he looked dead. Dead-dead, if you know what I mean."

"Who's Cy?"

"He was on Team Black and helped me find base. He was the one with the smoke bombs. I left him behind with my other friends."

"I hope they'll be okay."

"They'll take care of each other. We all want the same thing."

"To go home," Lila whispered.

"I'll help you get there. I promise."

Lila pulled back. "Thank you."

He stood awkwardly with her in his arms.

"You should put me down. You can't walk through these woods carrying me the whole time." Lila wiggled to make her point.

"There's no way you can walk without shoes, and you wouldn't have made it far in high heels anyway, so just say 'thank you, Ben' and enjoy the ride."

"I guess you're right," she reluctantly admitted, "but I don't want to be a burden, and it's not your job to take care of me."

Ben knew it wasn't, but in those few seconds after the words left her mouth, he wanted it to be. He wanted to take care of her, for the rest of his life.

When he didn't say anything, she changed the subject. "I missed you at the bar. I said something to Melanie and when I looked back, you were gone."

"I only stopped for a drink after working late. I didn't mean to stay for so long."

They fell silent, and Ben picked his way across the woods. The moonlight filtered through the branches, but the trees in places were thick and the light was almost nonexistent.

Ben knew women well enough to know Lila wasn't done. "You might as well say it."

She laughed and the tinkling sound echoed through the air. She clamped a hand over her mouth. "Do you think it's okay to make noise?"

Ben stopped and listened. He wasn't great with directions— not that he would admit it—but he was hoping he'd pointed them in the direction where Cy had pulled him from the door. If he made it back to that area, maybe he could find an entrance to the club.

The smoke bomb war's commotion faded, and there wasn't any noise besides a slight breeze rustling the trees, the branches scratching against each other, bare as old bones, like the ceramic skeleton his mother would hang from the door hook every Halloween.

He strained to hear a sound, any sound, and Lila held her breath. Her body's heat made his front warm but his back was freezing. He worried he wouldn't be able to bring her back to the club in time to prevent her from getting sick or frostbitten. He wanted to keep her safe. That was his one and only goal since finding her at the bonfire.

"I don't hear anything," he finally said.

That was worrisome in itself. He hadn't thought he walked far enough to distance themselves from the screams and gunshots between Team Black and the Camos. Sounds like that would carry, echo, maybe for miles, but no matter how hard he listened, only a crow in the distance pierced the silence.

Ben hefted her in his arms and started walking again. "I don't think anyone is after us."

"Is that good? That's good, right? Or not good? Should someone be looking for us?"

She sounded worried, and he hugged her closer. "I wouldn't mind seeing my friends, but with the way the Camos were playing, I don't want them looking for us. They didn't hurt you, did they?"

"No," she answered immediately. "They blindfolded me when we got to base, and tied me up, but the leader was very nice. He might have taken the game a little too seriously, though."

Ben snorted. "They all were."

He carried her a few more feet.

"I was going to say . . ."

Ben pulled his gaze off the forest debris as she leaned away to look up. Her lips trembled, maybe from nerves, but probably from the cold. Though they weren't in a great place right now, literally speaking.

He wasn't in a great place figuratively speaking either, his stare locked with hers. He was falling in love with her and she belonged to someone else.

"What?" he whispered, not wanting to break the spell that wove between them under a canopy of trees.

She lifted a hand to his cheek. "You seemed sad, at the bar."

There was no way he was having that conversation with her. There wasn't a point, and instead of replying, he kept walking.

Ben stumbled and righted himself before he dumped Lila to the ground. She squealed in surprise and tightened her grip around his neck.

"What the hell was that?" With Lila in his arms, he wasn't able to crouch down to investigate what tripped him. He carefully ran the toe of his shoe over the place he'd tripped. Wild grass, smaller branches, and stray pinecones hid the thick metal bar. He kicked it a ways, took a few steps in the opposite direction and found another one. "We're on an old train track."

"What does that mean?"

"It means—I'm not sure. These tracks haven't been used in a long time. I was thinking if we followed them . . . but if a railroad hasn't been using them, I don't know what we'd find, or how long it would take to find it."

"A better plan than nothing," Lila said hopefully.

"You think I didn't have a plan?" Ben teased, tightening his hold. She was small, but his arms were beginning to ache.

"You should put me down. I can walk."

"I'm not putting you down. The ground is covered with sticks and rocks and you're freezing." He paused. "Follow or not follow?"

"Follow." Lila sounded so sure he decided to take her lead.

"East or west?" If he'd had his phone with him, he could've used the compass in his Utilities app. He was all turned around and wasn't sure which direction he'd been walking all this time.

"Ummm, east."

That was opposite the direction his instincts told him to go, but he'd asked and would look like a jerk if he didn't do what she suggested.

He shuffled along the center the track, hoping they would find something before long. Stupid club. Maybe his fairy godmother would come rescue them. With everything he had experienced tonight, nothing seemed out of the realm of possibility.

Maybe they were still inside the club. That was stupid, he chastised himself, stepping over a larger tree branch. They were outside. They had to be. This forest was too real for it to a room inside a dance club. Besides, the Maze was in the middle of a city. He'd have to drive for hours to find woods this dense.

"What are you thinking?"

"Just wishing I knew where we were." Her voice trembled.

She was probably scared, and she didn't know him. He could be carrying her off to unspeakable things, and in The Maze, that didn't seem like such a farfetched scenario. "I won't hurt you. I would never hurt you, Lila. I swear."

She burrowed into his chest and gripped his shoulders. "I know. When you disappeared from the bar, I didn't think I would ever see you again. You paid in cash—there was no way for me to find you."

That pulled him up short, but before he could question her, they cleared a gathering of trees, and a huge cavern loomed in front of them. The mouth of the tunnel gaped pitch black, carved into a large . . . too big to be called a hill, too small to be called a mountain, the tunnel had been carved into the side of a . . . ridge. The tracks faded into the blackness, but he assumed they ran through the tunnel and came out the other side. "What do you think?"

She shrugged, her shoulder rubbing against his chest.

"This seems hopeless, either way."

He didn't want to, but he agreed with her.

Resigned, he kept moving and entered the mouth of the tunnel.

The darkness engulfed them, the tunnel ceiling shutting out what little moonlight had been guiding his footsteps.

His skin prickled with apprehension.

Being sheltered from the elements was a plus, however, and he relaxed slightly, warming up. Not a lot, but, as Lila said, it was better than nothing. Maybe they should try to make do here for the rest of the night and wait it out until morning.

The tunnel was just wide enough for a train to fit

through. The walls were smooth stone, and crush rock scattered along the ground. Ben was glad it was winter and most of the animals were hibernating or hiding from the cold. He wasn't much for bugs.

He tried squinting through the darkness, but he couldn't see anything and he didn't smoke leaving him without a lighter. The flashlight feature on his phone would have come in handy right about now. Damn, he didn't realize how many uses his phone had until he didn't have it.

His arms needed a rest, and he stopped and sat right where they were. Trying to find a comfortable place would have been fruitless. There were no soft places to sit.

Smoothing his hands over the ground, his hands brushed the wood from a rotted railroad tie and the cold rail under him, the metal digging into his ass.

Lila slid off his lap and settled next to him, pulling his jacket closer around herself.

Cy's flask clanked against the track as she shifted, and he thought maybe a sip or two would help warm them up a bit more. He reached around her for his jacket pocket, and her startled gasp echoed through the tunnel. Her breath fanned his cheek, the fruity hint of wine on her breath.

"Sorry," he muttered, pulling away, snagging the flask from his pocket. "Do you want a sip?"

"It wasn't you, I mean, it was you, but you surprised me, that's all."

"Don't worry about it." He nestled the flask in his lap, and he patted down her arms, finding her hands pulled inside his jacket's long sleeves. He pushed the flask into her grasp and when he was sure she had a good grip on it, he unscrewed the top for her.

The dark was disconcerting and made him uncomfortable. His eyes couldn't adjust to the poor light, because there wasn't any light at all. He had to rely on touch and hearing alone.

Lila felt around for his hand, and once she found it wrapped his fingers around the flask. Her touch made his heart beat heavier. He wanted her. "Thanks."

He took a sip of the whiskey and passed it back to her. The flask was almost full and would last them a long time if they took it easy. He'd have to be careful she didn't accidentally get drunk. They both needed to think clearly if they were going to get out of there without getting hurt.

"I was sad." The words slipped out. He hadn't meant to say them, but the silence could have been an excuse to hide, or an invitation to share.

She leaned into him and he wrapped his arm around her. "What happened?"

"I told Danny. He didn't tell you?" Ben felt silly for asking. They wouldn't have talked about him after he left.

Lila shook her head, moving against his shoulder.

"A few weeks ago my fiancée left me for another man. She'd been seeing him behind my back. I was stewing about it, I guess."

"Oh. I'm sorry."

She passed him the flask, and he screwed the little cap back on. He sat it on the ground next to him; it clanked against the train track when it fell over.

"It was for the best. We didn't love each other. She was just the one who admitted it first." He thanked Morgan for making him understand that.

"Still though. It's hard when a relationship ends. How long were you together?" She rushed on, "You don't have to answer that. It's too personal. Sorry."

"No. It's all right."

And it was. He liked sitting in the dark with her, talking, the warm buzz of whiskey warming his gut, loosening his tongue.

"It wasn't too long, actually. But to me it felt right. We were comfortable, never fought. Agreed on everything that mattered. It was like . . . living with my sister, or a friend. We had a camaraderie. Recently I was told that's not how I should have felt about her, and that's why she left. To find passion."

The metallic scent of rocks filled his nose, the mustiness of time gone by with no one to witness its passing.

"She found someone else and left." He hugged Lila closer, and he grazed his lips across her forehead, unable to stop himself. It didn't help she was so damn compliant because of the cold. "She found what she was looking for, and I've let her go. We're still friends. She left me her cat." Ben smiled against the top of Lila's head when she giggled. "How about you? How long have you and Danny been together?"

It felt natural to ask the question after telling her his story. He was glad he had decided to share, so he had the privilege of asking her questions in return.

"Danny?"

"Yeah. You two seem really close, and I saw how much he loves you. You guys are lucky. I want that, one day." Ben winced. That sounded like sappy drivel. Maybe he already had too much to drink.

"I suppose I am lucky," Lila agreed lightly, "but so's his wife."

Ben pulled away, appalled. "He's having an affair with you?"

Lila laughed, the pure sound of it ping-ponging against the tunnel walls like the little silver ball in a pinball machine. "No. Danny's my brother."

Ben's mouth fell open, and he was relieved Lila couldn't see the astounded look he knew to be on his face. Her brother. Fuck. He never thought that could have been a possibility. They had similar coloring, but never would he have put two and two together to actually get four.

"So who's the lucky man?" There had to be one; Lila was gorgeous and if he trusted his instincts, and his heart, he believed her to be a smart, funny, and kind woman.

"No one. My last relationship ended a while ago, and I've been enjoying being single, waiting for the right man to come along." She paused, sought his hand in the dark. "I met you in the bar and I was thinking maybe . . . but you seemed so sad, and when you up and left, I thought it was for the best."

"That's what I thought too. I thought you were with Danny and it was the right thing for me to do. To go. I didn't want to though."

Her hands fluttered along his suit, her fingers skimming his tie, snagging on his tie bar. She cupped his face as she had in The Lucky Clover and reached to place her lips on his. In the complete darkness, her aim was off and their noses bumped. He laughed and tilted his head so their lips met.

Their kiss was everything he knew it would be: warm, soft, and tasting of the whiskey from Cy's flask.

"Are you all right?" he asked after she pulled away.

"Yeah," Lila answered. "This isn't so bad after all."

He started to kiss her again only to stop, startled. "What was that?"

"I don't hear anything."

"Listen," he urged her.

Ben tilted his head, concentrating. The rumbling of a train locomotive, the distant shrill of a whistle. A train? His unspoken question was soon answered when the engine came into view as it followed the curve in the track.

After being in the dark for so long, the light from the engine blinded him.

"What's happening?" Lila asked confused.

"The train," Ben told her, tugging her to her feet. "There's a train on the tracks."

"I don't understand," she cried, running with him, stumbling over rocks and railroad ties.

Ben whirled on her, wasting precious seconds. "We're in the train's tunnel and there is no space for us to get out of the way. Do you get it now?" He searched her eyes, hating the panic and fear reflected in them.

The train barreled towards them, the light glaring in Ben's face. With the speed the train was traveling, and the distance they would have to run to clear the tunnel, they would never make it. To escape the cold he'd walked them in too far.

He wrapped his arms around her and held her close, giving up, because there was nothing else he could do. "I didn't think it would end like this."

He wouldn't make them try to run again, he wouldn't make them race the train. He would watch it come at them, watch his death with open eyes rather than get mowed down, his back turned.

"I was happy to have found you, for a little while."

The train's rumbling engine and shrieking whistle nearly drowned out her words. A plume of black smoke streamed from its chimney.

He buried his face in her hair; she hid her face against his chest. Ben prepared to be struck down as there was no other choice.

Giant gusts of wind billowed around them as the train

ghosted through their bodies. The force ripped Lila from his embrace, the wind clawing at him, snatching at his clothes, like little hands wanting any piece of him they could get.

Without warning, the wind stopped. His feet met solid ground. His head spinning, his stomach lurching, he gingerly opened his eyes.

CHAPTER FOUR

Five men sat around a poker table staring at him.

"Well? Are you gonna buy in or what?"

"What?" Ben blinked. He'd been prepared to die. The train had come straight at them. Frantically, he searched the room for Lila, but there was no bright green dress, no barefoot petite woman assuring him she was okay.

The man chomped on his cigar in frustration and annoyance. "You been standing there like an idiot for five minutes. Are you gonna buy in or what?"

A pedestal poker table covered in green felt sat under a naked bulb hanging from the ceiling. A bar made of red oak was positioned in the corner, and a cocktail waitress wearing a short black dress stood near it waiting for instruction.

There was no sign of Lila, and a huge pit formed in his stomach. He hoped she was safe, wherever she'd ended up. Now that he knew she wasn't with Danny and she wasn't dating anyone, he could find her after this ordeal was over, and maybe they would have a chance.

He sniffed his suit coat, and the material stank like smoke bombs.

The smoke bomb war had been real.

"I think you better have a seat."

A tall muscled man with blond hair pulled into a pony tail stood in the shadows of the room, and he pulled his jacket back to reveal his weapon shoved into the waistband of his pants.

Ben didn't like this. He was one hundred percent sure these men wouldn't let him leave if he didn't want to buy into their game.

He patted down his suit jacket, knowing he didn't have any cash on him. Anything he would've had left after paying for Lila's champagne at The Lucky Clover and his donation to Joe would have been in his wallet. In his jacket pocket. Which Lila still wore.

He shoved his hands into the pockets of his slacks. They were empty except for the gold coins he'd received from the trash receptacle. "All I have are these."

With a shaking hand, Ben pushed the gold coins onto the felt.

He needed a drink.

"Looks like this gentleman needs a drink!" the man with the cigar announced, eyeing Ben's trembling hand. He slammed his fist on the table making the colorful plastic chips rattle.

Stepping from the corner, the cocktail waitress approached him and shoved a snifter of a dark liquid at him.

Ben sniffed. Cognac. The good stuff. He drained the glass in two gulps.

"Get him another," the man shouted to the waitress. He addressed Ben, pointing to an empty chair with his smoking cigar. "Sit down. Your coins are a good buy-in. Very impres-

VANIA RHEAULT

sive. Don't wanna know where you got 'em, cuz I'm not gonna be responsible for what happens to you when they find out. We're playing Texas Hold 'Em."

Reluctantly, he lowered himself into a chair and kept his mouth shut. There was nothing wrong with those coins, and nothing was going to happen to him because he recycled a beer bottle.

If this guy thought he was going to intimidate him, he could think again. After what he'd faced tonight, a game of Texas Hold 'Em wasn't going to scare him. Even if he didn't know how to play poker. Didn't know Texas Hold 'Em from Blackjack, didn't know Blackjack from Old Maid.

And it didn't matter much, he'd lose his coins and be on his way. He didn't know how in the hell he ended up in this room, but he was damned glad his guts weren't spread all over a set of train tracks in the middle of nowhere.

He hoped she had made it back to the club, as he had.

At least, he assumed he was in the club, but one of his high school teachers told him what happened to people who assumed. Ben didn't like being called an ass.

The waitress pushed another snifter into his hand, this time half full.

He wasn't getting a good vibe from any of these men. In fact, one was so ashen, his skin was waxy like a corpse. He must have lost a shit-ton of money to look like that. Ben gulped, a sick feeling still roiling in his gut. He didn't like this at all.

Sweat rolled down his sides, and Ben swiped at his forehead with the back of his hand.

The dealer began distributing cards for a new hand.

The man with the ashen face swallowed thickly, as if trying not to throw up. The man with the cigar in his mouth, to Ben's right, rubbed his hands together with glee.

He must be winning. No one was that happy unless they were winning a hell of a lot of money.

The other men at the table were stoic, impassive. Maybe winners. Maybe losers. Maybe a little of both. Everyone was dressed in suits and there, at least, Ben felt as if he belonged. His Brooks Brothers suit had cost more than any suit had the right to cost, and he'd felt guilty, handing over his credit card when he knew the amount he was paying could feed a small country in Africa for a week.

These guys though, these guys all wore pinstripes. Pinstripes went out a long time ago. At least, he thought they had. Megan cared more about that stuff than he did. She had liked picking out his clothes, matching ties to his shirts.

When two men on his immediate right started betting, he bit back a curse. There weren't any cards on the table. This went against anything he knew about poker, which he'd learned watching *Ocean's Eleven*, and fuck, how long ago did that movie come out.

The man across the table from him carefully dealt each player two cards.

Everyone looked at their two cards, and Ben followed suit.

Betting began around the table.

The bet made its way to Ben, and he hunched over his cards while everyone glared waiting for him to say something. The man with the cigar came to his rescue, if Ben could call it that. "He's in and good for it."

Activity around the table resumed with the dealer sliding one card off the deck and putting it aside. Then he laid three cards in the middle of the table.

Ben didn't normally have a nervous tic, but his knee started to bounce up and down and he couldn't make it stop. He took another deep draw of his cognac which earned him odd looks. Maybe a person didn't drink while playing poker. Maybe a person needed to stay sober and keep their wits about them so they didn't go betting half-cocked, which apparently was easy to do if they fucking didn't know which cards they were gonna be able to use. Jesus Christ.

Another round of betting began, and Mr. Cigar made Ben's bet. He'd lucked out using that recycle bin. He would have been in a hell of a lot of trouble if he wouldn't have had those coins with him.

Corpse man ran from the room gagging, and to take his mind off the unease trailing an icy finger down his spine, Ben looked at his own cards. A Ten and a Jack.

Well, that was nothing.

The cards on the table were an Ace, a Two, and a Seven. Big deal.

More betting.

The dealer laid down another card. Queen.

More betting. Ben couldn't stop his knee from bouncing, but at least he didn't have anything in his pockets that rattled. That would have been as annoying as fuck, and probably not tolerated too well at the table, either.

Men raised, men folded.

The players remaining were himself, the dealer, and Mr. Cigar. Shit. He wanted to fold, but he didn't have a choice in the matter.

The dealer laid another card down on the green felt.

"Let's see 'em!" Mr. Cigar barked.

Ben threw his cards on the table. Thank God. He stood and smoothed his tie. "Gentleman, I'm sorry. It's been a pleasure," he lied. "Now I need—"

"Holy fuck!" Mr. Cigar stood slapped Ben heartily on the back.

The dealer groaned and threw his cards face down on the table.

"What?"

"A Royal Flush, you lucky son of a bitch. Rake it in!"

His Ten and Jack were lying near the Ace and the Queen. The last card the dealer had placed on the table had been a King.

He swallowed, afraid to touch the pile of chips. "All of it?"

"You bet, you lucky SOB," Mr. Cigar said around the cigar clamped between his teeth.

"Oh, okay. Thanks." Ben leaned over the table and pulled all the chips toward him. He wanted to get the hell out of there. "I appreciate the game, fellas, but I need to get going."

"Oh, I don't think so." Mr. Cigar's jovial tone disappeared. "I think you'll stay for another drink and another hand. Give us slobs the chance to win our money back."

The hulking bouncer shifted in the corner and met Ben's eyes. "Ah, right," he agreed, slowly returning to his seat.

Corpse never came back, and the game resumed without him.

Ben hadn't learned anything from his first hand and bet big in hopes of giving his pot away to the next winner.

His aim had narrowed.

He didn't want out of The Maze.

He wanted out of this room.

He tried, calmly, to place his cards on the table. Fewer players had opted to fold this hand, and his cards were horrible. Someone would have a better hand. He couldn't see how a Jack and a Seven would help him win a pile of rocks . . . unless the three cards he hadn't been paying attention to were also a Jack and two more Sevens.

Fuck.

"You son of a bitch," Mr. Cigar growled.

Before Ben could apologize for winning, Mr. Cigar pulled him from his chair and slammed him against the wall, one arm pinned between his shoulder blades, his face pressed uncomfortably against the cold surface.

He was a lot tougher than he looked, and Ben flinched when he whispered into Ben's ear, "We don't tolerate no cheaters here."

"But I didn't—"

"Oh no? Then what's this?"

He spun Ben around, throwing his suit coat open.

The guy with the gun who'd been standing in the corner reached into the inside pocket and pulled out an Ace of Hearts, holding it between his fore and middle finger, millimeters from Ben's nose.

Ben gaped. "I don't . . . I mean . . . I didn't . . ."

Mr. Cigar drew a pistol from the holster alongside his ribs and pressed it into Ben's gut.

He opened his mouth to once more plead his innocence, but Mr. Cigar didn't give him a second to explain. Without blinking, he pulled the trigger.

White heat spread throughout his entire body. He fell to the floor in agony, a moan trapped deep in his throat.

Mr. Cigar kicked him in the ribs, and all the agony blended together in a huge ball of excruciating fire.

"Let's get out of here."

Ben heard the voice over the loud buzzing in his ears. Feet scrambling against the floor, the bulb lighting the poker table blinked out, then there was nothing but silence.

This was different from the train.

When he'd held Lila, waiting to be plowed over, the idea of dying had been surreal, a dream. Never had he thought a train would kill him. Even when the light had been blinding, even when he could smell the smoke spewed by the engine's chimney, it hadn't felt real.

This was real. The blood seeping through his dress shirt was real.

The pain spread, the searing wound in his gut a glowing red hot poker being prodded into his skin.

He'd never been shot before. His father had never kept guns in the house while he was growing up. He didn't have cops for friends that he would visit at the station, didn't know any detectives who remained armed during their off duty times, he didn't hunt like Cy or shoot clay pigeons for fun.

Warm blood gushed through his fingers. It wasn't likely someone would find him before he died. He pictured himself in some abandoned warehouse on the docks, though he didn't hear any water. Maybe an old chop shop. Somewhere blue collar criminals hung out when they were done committing crimes for the day and needed to kick back and relax.

He held his breath, but he didn't hear anything except the blood rushing in his ears as his heart pumped it from his body.

He was letting his mind get away from him. He needed to think. Think about something important. People maybe. He thought about his parents; he wouldn't get a chance to tell them goodbye. Megan. He wanted to tell her to come back and pick up her cat. He wouldn't be able to take care of Tabby anymore. Moaning, he rolled over onto his back.

Lila.

He'd been goddamned surprised Danny was her brother, that she had been looking for him after he left her brother's bar. He'd miss her, and the future they could have had together.

The pain became unbearable, and Ben gratefully let himself be swept away by the blackness.

Shouting and a loud bang jolted Ben awake. Two men dressed in white down to their tennis shoes, pushed a gurney, laughing. Their passenger moaned a deep guttural groan that made his skin crawl.

A thin ribbon of blood dripped from the fingertips of the patient covered by thin blue blanket that had seen better days.

One orderly asked, "Why can't Miss Piggy count to seventy?"

"Why?" the other asked, grinning.

"Because when she gets to sixty-nine she always has a frog in her throat!"

The two men laughed maniacally and disappeared around the corner, smearing the trail of blood with their shoes.

Their laughter faded, leaving Ben alone.

In the silence, the nightmare came crashing down and urgently he patted his abdomen. He stifled a groan when his fingers met the sticky blood on his shirt and the swollen, tender wound beneath his clothes.

He closed his eyes and blew out a breath. Mr. Cigar had really shot him, and without medical attention, he was fucked. He wasn't likely to find a doctor in The Maze, or wherever the hell he was now.

He'd held on to a hope that he'd see Lila again, but that was just a fantasy now. Defeated, he eased his eyes open. At least he could get a look at the place where he would die. His vision wavered, and he blinked, then blinked again.

Illuminated by bright lights, fish swam above him, immersed in crystal clear water. They were lazily moving their fins, as if they had nowhere to go, and were in no hurry to get there.

Enormous sharks floated along, their grins displaying white sharp teeth, their silver eyes flat. He lay there, mesmerized, until a huge brown scaly reptile-like creature slithered above him. The creature was so huge Ben couldn't see what it was, but unable to tear his eyes away, he stared until the reptile floated from sight.

The shimmering water made eerie bluish patterns on the plain white wall, and trying to roll to his side, he realized he was lying on a gurney as well. His movements were restricted by a pulling at his wrist.

Medical tape held an IV in place, and the tube was connected to a plastic bag, its contents a golden yellow. It looked like piss, but the pain was gone and he was feeling woozy, so he gave the bag the benefit of the doubt.

Ben was about to pull out his IV and search for help when the faint tap of heels stopped him.

A woman, flanked by two orderlies who were dressed similarly as the other two who had pushed the gurney past him moments before, clicked her way down the hall. Her white heels matched her white pantyhose and little white dress. A nurses' white hat perched on her head, a big red cross in the center.

She grinned around a lollipop's white stick poking from between her lips. Her lips were painted with the same shade of red as the cross on her hat.

The nurse jogged his memory, and when she smiled at him, he recognized her face and her short curly platinum hair. "Aren't you the cigarette girl from earlier?"

"I don't know what you're talkin' about," she said in the high pitched nasally voice Ben remembered. "Dollface, you must be higher than a kite from all these pain meds. I don't even smoke, baby."

Her breath smelled like cherries, her teeth tinged pink from the candy in her mouth. Her eyes were wide and blue, framed with thick black lashes. She leaned over him until she was almost on top of him to whisper in his ear, "We need to get you out of here. They're prepping surgery for you now, sweet pea."

Oh, hell, no. He didn't want someone cutting into him. Especially not from anyone at this hospital. But one of the orderlies pulled his rolling IV stand, the other pushed his bed, and the nurse gripped his hand.

Ben *did* feel muzzy from the medication, if that's what it was, and he didn't know how long he'd been out. He could have been unconscious for days.

He rubbed his face with his free hand until he was forced to hold on. The orderlies pushed the gurney faster and faster, the nurse giggling with delight and skipping to keep up. They took a corner so fast Ben would have been flung onto the dirty floor if not for the gurney's rail.

They skidded to a stop in front of a large elevator, and Ben sat up, almost pulling the IV out of his arm.

The nurse jabbed her finger at the UP arrow button and pushed him back down, glaring.

"Hey, I wanted to push the button."

"No, you got to push the button last time. It's my turn."

The nurse pulled the lollipop out of her mouth. "It was my turn to push the button and I already did, so shut the hell up."

Before the two men replied, the elevator doors swooshed open.

"Get our patient inside before he bleeds to death!" she growled, but it came out more as a squeal, and she poked one of the orderlies in the chest with a fingernail painted blood red. "You know Dr. Romano don't like waiting around."

The two clowns bumped Ben back and forth as they maneuvered the large gurney and IV pole into the elevator. Feeling too vulnerable and helpless, he wished he could sit up or walk himself to the operating room. Even a wheelchair would have been better than this. Flat on his back, all he could do was stare at the ceiling of the elevator, fluorescent lights casting a sickly yellowish blue color over all of them.

Music piped into the rectangular box from hidden speakers, the jarring notes of Queen's "Another One Bites The Dust." That wasn't a good sign, though after all he had been through tonight, he was amazed he wasn't already dead.

The elevator doors slid open with a hiss and the orderlies pushed Ben into a bright hallway. Padded handrails lined the corridor, and an old woman shuffled along, gripping it for dear life.

Now *this* was what a hospital was supposed to feel like, and Ben relaxed. No fish swimming above him, no concrete flooring as if he were in someone's basement, or the morgue. No creepy music. Perfectly norm—

The orderlies pushed him past a nurses' station. The group of women weren't reading charts, they weren't conferring with doctors or even talking amongst themselves. They were . . .

Holy crap.

Ben propped himself on his elbows to get a better look over the silver rail of the gurney. Dressed in scrubs and tennis shoes—unlike the pinup nurse still at his side—they exercised in an aerobic session led by Richard Simmons. He'd covered his frizzy, curly hair with swim cap covered with brightly colored plastic flowers, and he wore a skin-tight, hot pink tank top tucked into the smallest pair of black spandex shorts.

Richard shuffled in a dance movement, and when he looked over his shoulder, blew Ben a kiss and gave him a little finger wave before leading the class in another move.

A deep ache pounded his head, and he slumped onto his pillow.

The orderlies shoved the gurney through two wide doors marked OR.

His throat closed up, and he started to sweat. There was no way in hell he was going to let anyone in this place operate on him. He'd get out of this hellhole or die trying, and he was peeling the tape off his IV when a familiar voice soothed his soul like aloe on a burn.

"Well, Benjamin Langdon! Aren't you a sight for sore eyes!"

The orderlies wheeled his gurney under the bright light in the center of the room. Trays lined with blue paper held scalpels of many sizes, sponges, and other paraphernalia doctors used in surgeries.

VANIA RHEAULT

"Felix," Ben rasped in relief. His friend would help get him out of there.

"Here's your patient Dr. Romano," the nurse screeched, flicking the lollipop stick on the floor.

Dr. Romano? Felix wasn't a doctor. He owned a freaking car dealership.

"Thank you, nurse," Felix replied, wrapping his arms around her. He pulled the nurse closer and gave her a deep French kiss. She reciprocated, twisting her fingers in his hair.

Felix pushed her away. "Mmmm," he hummed and smacked his lips. "Cherry. My favorite. Now get out of here, I have work to do." He slapped her ass, and she giggled scooting away.

The doors hit the walls with a loud bang as the nurse and the orderlies slammed out of the operating room. The three ran down the hallway, hooting like little kids after being let out of school on the last day before summer vacation.

Ben breathed a sigh of relief. Now things would get back to normal.

Felix caught a stool on wheels with his foot and dragged it over to Ben's gurney. He sat down and lifted Ben's shirt to inspect the gunshot wound.

"Got yourself into some trouble, didja?" Felix asked, prodding the hole in Ben's gut. The wound still oozed blood, and a pain shot through his torso.

Wincing, he pulled away. "*Doctor* Romano?"

Felix shrugged. "You can be whatever you want in The Maze."

"And you wanted to be a doctor? You never told me that," Ben said, scowling. "I thought we told each other everything."

Felix laughed, but it didn't help ease his tension. It wasn't a good laugh. Not the carefree laugh he was used to from his friend.

"Not out there, moron. In here. In The Maze. The doctor and the hot nurses? That just ain't rumor my friend. I save lives and my nurses show their appreciation in a method I fully encourage. Bedside manner is not lacking, my man, not with my ladies."

He didn't care who Felix screwed. He was about to say so when Felix said, "You've been a bad boy, Ben."

"What do you mean?"

The whole situation made him uneasy and he wanted to sit up, wanted to be on an even level with his friend. But the flinty look in Felix's eyes warned him to play it cool because something wasn't right.

"You got Simon's call, didn't you?" Felix asked.

"Yeah. It's what brought me here."

"Did you find them?"

Felix cleaned Ben's wound with a warm cloth. It only took a few seconds for the white cloth to turn red from the dried crusted blood that coated Ben's skin.

"Yeah. They'd gotten sucked into this weird game of Flag. It was strange, man. I was with this guy, and I think he shot someone. Like dead." Ben squirmed. He didn't like the cloth near his wound. It felt like little worms digging their way under his skin.

Felix's blue eyes were chiseled ice, and Ben didn't want to risk telling him to stop. This wasn't his friend. Felix didn't act this way. He wouldn't impersonate a doctor. He didn't treat women like pieces of tail. He certainly wouldn't look at Ben the way he was now, like he would rather kill him than help him.

"Where are they now?"

Ben met Felix's cold gaze. "What do you mean?"

"Where are they now? Kip? Alan? Simon? Even poor Cy. You found them, and then what?"

His stomach sank. Felix knew he'd abandoned his friends in the woods.

"And then you saved the girl, isn't that right, Ben? You left the boys in a smoke bomb war where they could have gotten shot. To save the girl."

Felix's gentle movements weren't gentle any longer.

"They were having a good time." While it was true Simon, Kip, and Alan had been having a good time throwing smoke bombs, Felix was right. He'd even worried about it while carrying Lila through the woods. Those guns had been real.

"Ben, Ben, Ben," Felix said, shaking his head. "Bros before hos, isn't that what we've always said?"

Ben was tired of this. He peeled the tape off his wrist and pulled the thick needle from underneath his skin leaving a small purple hole that oozed blood.

"Felix, you're full of shit. We've never said that, not once. It sounds like something stupid from *One Tree Hill*, which was actually a decent show for a couple of seasons. Listen, I'm sorry I left them behind, but she needed help, and I wasn't going to sit around and let her get hurt in the fight." He tried to sit up, but Felix pushed him back.

"I can't let you leave yet, Benji Boy. You have a hole in your stomach, or did you forget? You have a bullet in your gut, and we need to pull it out and sew you up. Now lie back real nice, and let me help you out."

Ben wasn't going to let Felix touch him anymore. He had no more medical training than the janitor in Ben's office complex. "Calm down and fuck off. I'm going home."

Four orderlies dressed like circus clowns in bright red

jumpers, white face makeup, wide red smiles, and green hair rushed into the operating room, circled his bed, and held him down.

Ben struggled, frantic. He kicked out, but his gunshot wound made him weak. He was no match for the burly clowns.

"*You* calm the fuck down," Felix snarled, leaning into Ben's face. Felix reached above his head and pulled down a clear plastic mask.

One orderly held Ben's head in a vise-like grip, and Felix placed the plastic cup over Ben's nose and mouth. "Now settle down. You won't feel a thing. Count backwards from ten, Benji Boy, and when you wake up it will be all over."

Ben tried to hold his breath but it was no use. His body craved air and he deeply inhaled.

The last thing he heard before blacking out was Felix announcing, "I'm gonna go watch some football."

CHAPTER SIX

Ben awoke with a start and jackknifed into a sitting position. He braced for the onslaught of the next room.

This room was dark but for the glow of a computer monitor. The smell of old books and dust met his nose. Only the tick, tick, ticking of a wall clock pierced the silence.

He forced himself to relax and dragged in slow, deep breaths, willing his racing heart to slow down. Perspiration drenched his skin, and spots danced in his vision. He rested a cheek against the fuzzy soft material of the loveseat he'd been sleeping on.

Memories assailed him, and Ben shoved his hands beneath his shirt, searching for the gunshot wound.

There was nothing.

In disbelief, he pushed his shirt aside and angled himself to catch the bluish glow of the computer monitor, white clouds floating through a blue sky, the screensaver doing its job.

His stomach was fine.

Ben inspected his wrist. There was no telltale sign of an

IV. No bruising, no small hole. He stiffened when the door creaked open, and he prepared to bolt when an older man dressed in black filled the doorway.

"I'm not going to hurt you."

After this bizarre night, he wasn't about to believe that, and he sat on the edge of the sofa, his hands clenched into fists.

"I'm Father Tim. I'm the priest here at St. Joseph's Church."

Ben ran his tongue over his teeth. The inside of his mouth tasted like the paper mâché paste he ate in first grade. "I'm in a church? This isn't The Maze?"

Father Tim leaned against the doorframe, crossing his arms and ankles. "Is that where you've been?"

He sounded slightly disapproving, but Ben didn't blame him. He didn't think a priest would condone any part of what went on in a club like The Maze.

"No wonder you look worse for wear."

"How did I get here?"

Father Tim sat in the desk chair near the computer. "Joe found you wandering outside without a jacket. When he brought you here to get you out of the cold, he showed me the card you had given him, and the money." He paused. "What was a man of your character doing in a place like that?"

Ben loosened his hands and shook them out, his knuckles cracking. He chuckled wryly. "I answered a call from a friend saying he needed help. I didn't even know where I was until I stepped inside. Not my kind of place, believe me, and after tonight, I won't ever be going back."

Father Tim laughed. "Were you able to help them?"

Felix's accusations rang in his head. "Kind of," he

admitted now. He wasn't Catholic but he felt a strong urge to confess.

Father Tim didn't seem concerned. "In a place like that, that's probably the best you could hope for."

"Maybe you're right."

If Father Tim wasn't going to condemn him, maybe he shouldn't condemn himself, because in all honesty, he didn't know the real from the fake.

Lila.

He should have protected her. He should have been man enough to help her escape. Instead he'd allowed the train to rip her from his arms. He didn't know if she'd made it safely home or if he would see her again. She probably hated him now. He'd been weak, like all the princes the Evil Queen told him about.

He'd failed.

"You said Joe brought me here? Where is he?"

"He's sleeping. You were lucky he was still out in the streets."

"Yeah, I am. What time is it?" Ben was bone weary and his head throbbed.

"Almost six in the morning. You've been here a couple of hours. Let me call you a cab. Do you need cab fare?" Father Tim asked, tilting his head in compassion.

Heat creeped up Ben's neck. He stood and shoved his hands into the pockets of his dress slacks. "Y—" He stopped when his fingers closed around a cell phone. "I thought this was stolen," he said, surprised, pulling it out and turning it over in his hands. "A woman pick-pocketed me and took it from my jacket pocket. How in the hell did I get it back?" Ben winced. "Sorry."

Father Tim shook his head. "No problem. I've been known to say the same thing a time or two. Let me call you a cab and give you fare. It's the least I can do after you befriended Joe as you did."

Ben turned on his phone, and a blank home page filled the screen. He didn't have any text messages and no one had tried to call him. His battery life was near full. He popped the phone from the case and peeled a fifty dollar bill from the sleek back of the phone where he kept it for an emergency.

"Thanks, but that's okay. I've got a bit of cash here and I can call. I appreciate you putting me up for a while, and thank Joe for helping me out. I don't remember him helping me walk here."

"You were mumbling something about getting shot. I checked you over and didn't find anything that warranted immediate attention, or I would have called an ambulance instead of letting you sleep."

Father Tim led Ben through the huge run-down church, the sanctuary dark but for several candles lit near the altar, and into the church's thinly carpeted foyer. Benches lined the walls and a coat closet sat off to the side.

"But," Father Tim continued, "you may have been drugged. I would get looked at tomorrow. Just to be sure."

Ben nodded.

"I need to get back," the priest said apologetically. "My deacon is waiting for me. We have Saturday morning mass soon, such as it is. Every year my congregation grows that much smaller."

Sticking a hand out for him to shake, Ben said, "Thanks again. If, ah, you need help around here, or Joe . . ." He shrugged, uncomfortable. "Joe has my card."

Father Tim's mouth quirked in a smile. "I'll take you up on that. Don't be a stranger, Ben. Joe took a liking to you."

With that, Father Tim returned to the sanctuary,

leaving Ben alone in the foyer. The sun hadn't yet risen, and Tiffany lamps sitting on small end tables lit up the church's lobby.

Ben used his phone to find the number for a taxi company and called for a pick up.

While he waited, he thought about Lila. He only knew how to find her through her brother's bar. He would sleep off tonight and go to The Lucky Clover and talk to Danny. Maybe the bartender would tell him how to get a hold of her. Maybe she would leave a message for him there.

The ride home flew by in a sleepy blur.

As the driver of the yellow taxi drove away, Ben stood in front of his little blue house. He would sell it. He didn't know if a future was in the cards for him and Lila, but he wouldn't ask her to live here when he'd shared his bed with another woman.

The stars were still twinkling in the winter sky, lights dotted the neighborhood with early morning risers, and he was more tired than he'd ever been. He was so exhausted it didn't register that the knob of his front door twisted easily in his hand until he'd stepped inside.

The miraculous scent of coffee nearly drove him to his knees—and brought him up short. Someone was in his house.

He took off his shoes in the entryway and hung his suit coat in the closet near the door.

Cautiously, his shoulders tense, he walked through the laundry room to the kitchen, preparing for a fight, ready for whatever had followed him home from The Maze.

She was sitting at his little round table, holding onto a mug of coffee, the tea lights Megan left behind in the center of the table flickering prettily, the only light in the room. She had let her hair down, thick black curls swirling around her shoulders. The bow of her dress had come undone and the ribbon trailed down to the floor, where Tabby batted at the ends.

"How did you get in?"

Stupid question. He knew it when the words left his mouth, but her presence was a mystery and gift rolled into one. He wanted the answers, but only because he wanted her there, wanted her in his life, and he didn't want it to be a mistake . . . or a dream.

Or another room.

Lila dangled his keyring from her fingers.

"But how did you know where I live?" he pressed.

He couldn't get over her sitting at his kitchen table. He couldn't get over how her eyes glittered in the candles' flame. He couldn't get over how much he'd missed her, how much he'd worried about her, or how much he knew he could love her.

Lila nodded to his wallet that sat on the table near the candles. "I found your driver's license. I hope you don't mind." She pulled a face. "I paid for a taxi with some cash from your wallet. I didn't know what else to do. I never made it back to the coat check to grab my jacket. I can pay you back."

Ben took a tentative step toward the kitchen table. They didn't know each other well, and he didn't know what she had gone through at the club without him. "I don't mind. You don't have to pay me back. Lila, you could have gone home."

The question was implied. And he waited for an answer.

Lila stood and took a step toward him; she still wasn't wearing shoes. "I didn't want to go home. I wanted to see you." Her voice grew husky with tears. "Oh, God, Ben, I was so worried about you. Wh-what happened to you after the train?"

"Nothing I want to talk about now. Lila, you're okay?" Ben couldn't stay away from her a moment longer, and he picked her up and sat her on the island in the middle of the kitchen, bringing her face to face.

Her mascara was a bit smeared, her lipgloss entirely gone. Dark circles rested beneath her eyes. She was beautiful.

She nodded, and he searched her eyes for the truth. He saw it there, along with fatigue . . . and an expression Megan had never worn when she looked at him.

Passion.

Lila pulled on his tie and pressed her lips against his. He cradled her face in his hands, rubbing his thumbs along her jaw. He angled his head and pulled her closer, and she wrapped her arms around his neck.

Reluctantly, Ben pulled away. "Are you tired, sweetheart?" he asked, though it was obvious she was. He was too. They had both been awake all night.

She rested her head on his shoulder. "Yeah, I am. Can I stay?"

Ben held her against his chest, the very same way he had walking her through the woods. "Do you want to?"

Lila nodded against his shoulder, and her head grew heavy, her body loosening in sleep as he carried her upstairs to the master bedroom.

"You can stay, Lila. You can stay, for the rest of your life, if you'd like."

Instead of pulling the blankets back, he laid her on top of them, and she burrowed her head into one of his pillows. As she rolled to her side, he covered her with a thick throw folded at the foot of the bed.

Ben rounded the mattress and crawled next to her.

As he spooned her, she reached for his hand and tucked it under her cheek.

The sun began to rise, and the weak light cast her skin in a rosy pink. He drank her in, one last glimpse of her before his eyelids closed in sleep.

This was love, this was passion. Morgan was right. To try to live without it was foolish.

He found it, with Lila, all because of a call that had brought him to 1700 Hamilton.

EPILOGUE

"It still seems like a dream sometimes."

"I don't know what else it could have been."

They were walking downtown, toward The Maze.

Winter had given up and a warm breeze blew, Lila's hair fluttering around her shoulders and down her back. Ben gripped her hand and the diamond of her engagement ring bit into the side of his finger. He didn't mind.

They didn't speak much of their time after the train had torn them apart. The dance club never returned Lila's coat, and she had been forced to replace her cell phone. Ben didn't mind that either. They were on a family plan now, and happiness turned up the corners of his mouth.

A couple of days after that night, Ben called Alan, Kip, and Simon. They'd made it out of the smoke bomb war just fine, and Cy, too. Ben asked them all to be groomsmen in his wedding and invited them to an engagement party so they could meet Lila properly. They accepted, and Simon promised Lila he wouldn't order any smoke bombs for the reception.

Ben saved Felix for last. He didn't know what to say to

his friend, and he was surprised one afternoon to find Felix at the doorstep of his and Lila's new house, a bouquet of roses for her, a bottle of Jameson and a huge apology for him.

He had gotten swept up in The Maze he said, and he was sorry.

The anesthesia had ultimately sent Ben to Father Tim's church, and it would have been difficult for him to ignore the apology.

Plus, he liked Jameson. A lot.

And he needed a best man.

At Lila's insistence, after coffee and visiting with Danny, they walked to The Maze and stood outside the front of 1700 Hamilton for the first time since that night. It looked different in the daylight. Like any other building in the poorer section of the business district.

Lila leaned against the light post, the one that had been dark, and still was for all Ben knew. "We can't hate the place," she said.

They had this conversation all the time, talking about their love-hate relationship with the club.

Ben rested an arm against the faded green post and cupped her cheek in his palm. He would never tire of looking at her. "No," he agreed, "I'll never truly hate it, because it brought me you, but I'll never go in there again."

He bent to kiss her, but he paused. "There is one thing I keep forgetting to ask about that night."

"Oh, yeah? What's that?"

"How did you walk across the grating in your high heels?"

The question had bothered him at the time, and now, looking at The Maze, he remembered to ask.

Lila laughed and gave Ben a smacking kiss on his lips. "It must have been magic."

On the Corner
of
Hamilton and Main

CHAPTER ONE

The door of The Lucky Clover closed with a soft thump behind Lila Donahue, and she gratefully stepped into the warmth of the bar. Too bad her friend Brigid couldn't be like other brides and marry in the spring.

Her friends chattered and laughed their way to the wall of banquettes, and she followed them, soaking in the heat, goosebumps rising over her skin. Danny stood behind the bar wiping the spotless bar top. Lila didn't need to see the polished oak to know it already gleamed. The Lucky Clover was Danny's pride and joy.

A man hunched over his drink while Danny spoke to him, though it didn't look like the gentleman in the black suit coat cared to be drawn into conversation.

Trailing behind her friends, Lila took off her jacket revealing her short green dress. Searching the racks at her favorite department store, it had been love at first sight. The green brought out her eyes, and she adored the big floppy bow at the back of her neck. Even buying it from the petite department the dress had needed hemming, but that wasn't anything new.

Lila shoved her jacket onto the banquette bench. The static electricity shocked her fingertips and her dress clung to her legs. She smoothed the material over her hips and down her thighs before she ran across the black carpeting and hoisted herself onto the bar as she always did when she visited Danny. Her legs dangled, the tips of her sandals bumping against the wood.

The man nursing a glass of something amber looked at her, but before she could greet him, Danny leaned across the bar and gave her his customary smack on the lips.

She hoped he didn't smear her lipgloss.

"You're here for the party, then, lass," Danny said in his fake Irish brogue that never failed to amuse her. While she and Danny were indeed Irish, neither of them had ever set foot in Ireland and didn't have any plans to do so, either.

She laughed. "Yes! You know it's Brigid's bachelorette party."

After telling Danny of Brigid's upcoming nuptials he invited them to come and drink their first round of toasts at the bar.

She couldn't very well refuse a man so close to her heart. Besides, sitting in Danny's quiet bar was certainly a step up from anywhere else they would likely go. So much a homebody was she, her friends routinely called her a recluse and all around stick-in-the-mud.

"Aye, Brigid. A fine young lad finally captured her heart."

Lila laughed again, rolling her eyes, his accent sounding charming and ridiculous at the same time.

Danny was dressed in his usual bartending uniform: a black vest, red tie, and bright white dress shirt. His blue eyes glowed with humor, his mouth stretched into a teasing smile.

She loved this man. She really did.

"You're not leaving us already? You oughtn't leave me alone with this group!" Danny protested suddenly to the stranger, and for the first time since perching on the bar, Lila allowed herself to get a good look at the man seated next to her.

He wore a suit coat that screamed money, the black and grey tie alone probably costing as much as a bottle of the champagne her friends wanted to drink.

But it wasn't the suit or the tie that captivated her, it was the sad, lost look in his dark coffee-colored eyes.

The smile he gave Danny was wistful and complemented the lonely look. "That isn't a hardship."

Lila's eyes met the stranger's and her breath hitched.

He stared at her, and she couldn't look away. Under the sadness something smoldered, a smoke, rising to the surface.

Danny smirked, his eyes darting between them, and, mercilessly, he would tease her later. Always one to be choosy, being caught up in a stranger's gaze wasn't like her, and Danny would take the opportunity to poke at her.

She gathered her wits and remembered her manners. "Hi."

"Hello."

Lila melted at the gentleman's greeting. Rough, smoky, like the shadows in his eyes, but smooth, his voice rich, like the best whiskey she was sure Danny was serving him.

It would be lovely to hear that voice in the middle of the night, his lips pressed against her ear, his warm breath tickling her skin.

Um.

Needing to fill the awkward silence, she swung her legs as was her custom.

Swing, bang, swing, bang.

Danny gestured with his rag, flopping it between them. "This is . . ."

"Benjamin. Ben," he said, and Lila settled her feet onto the golden foot rest that ran along the bottom of the bar.

Ben held out his hand and the size and warmth engulfed her palm and fingers. Her hands were still chilled. Lila had forgotten her gloves at home, not that it mattered much. Walking downtown in a short dress and sandals was a recipe for a frozen disaster.

Unable to resist the look in his eyes or the heat of his skin, she pulled her hand from his, and in a bold move not like her, cupped his face in her hands. Never before had she been so forward, or wanted to be, but something in this man called to her. Something made her want to take him home, crawl into his lap and promise to make it all better.

To hide her feelings, she said cheerfully, "I bet you were a Benji at school."

Lila laughed in delight when he blushed, clearly befuddled. He was handsome, his dark brown hair gleaming, the stubble on his jaw past being called a five o'clock shadow.

Ben cleared his throat, and even that sounded sexy. "How did you know?"

"Because you are so freaking adorable!"

And he was. Lila would bet he had women crawling all over him since, well, since he could crawl. The sadness, the mystery, only added to his appeal.

Her friends started shouting at her. "Come on, Lila. We want the booze!"

Lila inwardly grimaced. She loved her friends, but oh, going home with this man, to offer him the comfort he seemed he needed, was a much better alternative to anything else her friends could think of to celebrate Brigid's last week of freedom.

She tried to sound happy. "I'm coming!"

Lila pulled her hands away from Ben's face, his stubble deliciously scraping her fingertips. Sh wanted to know what his stubble feel like against her lips.

"So you came in to use me for me booze," Danny moaned.

Lila stifled a snort. "You knew we were coming in," she reminded him playfully, forcing herself to grin.

"Aye," Danny agreed, his eyes downcast, his lips shaped into a sad frown.

An actor to the last, was Danny.

"This doesn't seem the best place to party."

Lila studied the bar through Ben's eyes.

The leather and wood, the fake plants in the corners that added the only color to the décor. A faint tinkling of piano keys drifted from hidden speakers.

It was a fine place to drink for those who didn't want to deal with a crowd, loud music, or silly cocktails called Blowjobs and Sex on the Beach. Danny's bar was classy, elegant, much like the man himself. Sure, the bar didn't attract much traffic on a Friday night at nine, but Sunday through Thursday the place was full to bursting with men and women alike who wanted a quiet place to nurse a glass of wine or a bottle of something old.

"Oh, it's not," she agreed with Ben. This place was the last place she would choose to party, if she liked doing such things, but she spent many an hour sipping coffee, reading and keeping Danny company on quiet nights like this. She loved it. "But Danny told us to come in for a couple bottles and I can never say no to him."

Danny winked at Ben. "I wanted the company."

Lila knew he did. Some nights he didn't have one customer. Danny spent plenty of time reading as well.

Danny reached below into the cooler for the bottles of champagne he'd set aside for her friends.

Ben started to put his jacket on and Lila bit back a moan of dismay.

"Don't go yet," she pleaded impulsively, and she inwardly cringed at her carelessness.

Lila hid her embarrassment by wiggling onto the stool next to his, sitting on a hip so she could rest her elbow on the bar, supporting her head in her hand. She placed her other hand on the back of her stool and crossed her legs feigning a nonchalance she was far from feeling.

She was nervous! When had talking to a man made her sweat like this? She hoped the darkness of the bar hid the sweat stains she was sure were forming in the material of her dress.

He seemed surprised she'd asked him to stay, but he let his jacket fall from his grasp and hang on the back of his stool.

Eager to make conversation now she had his full attention, she asked the first thing that came to her mind. "How did you find this place?"

He smoothed his jacket on the backrest so it wouldn't fall to the floor. It looked soft and warm, and she bet it held the lingering scent of his aftershave.

"I was walking home from work and here it was. Decided to pop in for minute and here I am." He paused. "It doesn't seem as if this place gets much business."

Maybe she didn't seem like such a big fool as she felt she was acting. She laughed, relieved. Maybe she was making a better impression than she thought.

"We do all right."

She didn't know where the "we" came from. She didn't have anything to do with The Lucky Clover since it had opened besides helping Danny count bottles during inventory.

Her friends hooted when Danny popped the corks on their champagne bottles. That was another reason her friends wanted to drink here. Not only was the booze free, her friends loved looking at Danny. Though he was taken, it didn't stop them from drooling.

"You're missing all the action," Ben noted.

"So I am, but the night is young and I'm afraid I have many hours of this to go." Many, many hours, and Lila held in a sigh, blinking, forcing herself to keep eye contact under his scrutiny.

"You don't like to party?" he asked curiously.

Oof. If he could hear her reluctance, she better adjust her attitude. She should try, at least, so Brigid would have a good time.

"Not so much," she admitted, trying not to care if she sounded boring. She wasn't twenty-one anymore and there was more to a good time than booze and deafening music. "But it's a special night for Brigid and we started here to ah, prime the pump, as you say, for free. Danny won't charge us for the bottles."

No, her friends wouldn't let her miss a night like this. Brigid was ecstatic her boyfriend finally popped the question.

Danny was thrilled too and asked Lila to come in and celebrate with him. What she told Ben true—she could never say no to Danny. Fake Irish accent or no, he was the light of her life.

"He's a nice guy," Ben commented.

Her friends grew louder with every sip and she was being rude talking to Ben instead of sitting with them. Sure, Danny was keeping them occupied, but she was

Brigid's maid of honor and she shouldn't be ignoring the bride.

Reluctantly, Lila held out her hand. She would figure out a way to slip him her phone number. She wanted to see him again, get to know him, erase the shadows in his brown eyes. "It was nice meeting you. Don't be a stranger, Ben."

He frowned at her, and when he didn't take her hand, she slipped off the barstool, hurt and confused. Maybe he wasn't interested.

Win some, lose some. She fought a burn in the back of her throat. This was definitely a loss.

She slid into the banquette next to Melanie and took a sip of the champagne waiting for her.

Danny left them to celebrate and took his position behind the bar.

"Who's that hunky guy you were talking to?" Melanie asked, on her way to becoming quite tipsy. Melanie had never referred to a guy as 'hunky' in all her life.

She balanced on a hip on the bench cushion, her legs crossed underneath the table. "His name is Ben. I think he's been talking to Danny for a while."

"He's gorgeous." Melanie giggled and covered a hiccup with her hand. "You should give him your phone number. Go, do it now." She pushed Lila on her shoulder.

Lila shook her head. Melanie, a blonde Southern belle who moved north for school and never went back, was the most romantic of the bunch. Lila bet Melanie would like nothing more than for her to get picked up by a Prince Charming in a bar.

A gust of cold air chilled Lila and she squeaked in dismay. "Oh, no. No," she whispered. "Ben!"

His barstool was empty, and Danny pushed a key, popping his register open.

"Oh, no." She scurried out of the banquette and ran across the bar. "Where did he go?" she cried to Danny startling him with her outburst.

Danny slammed the register shut. "He paid for your champagne and took off." His Irish accent was gone. "What's this now? You took a fancy to him?"

Lila stood on the footrest near the register. "Yeah. Kind of." She rested her head on her arms. "What's his last name?" she asked excitedly, pleased she thought of it. "On his credit card slip, or his check. I can look him up online."

Danny was shaking his head before she'd finished speaking. "He paid in cash, darling. I'm sorry."

Lila narrowed her eyes. "You don't sound sorry. What did he tell you?"

"That is a bartender-client privilege, young woman," Danny reminded her.

Many of his clients told Danny their drunken secrets, and he divulged not a one.

"I'm never going to see him again," Lila wheedled, though her heart sank at the thought.

Danny's lips thinned in disapproval. "You know I have more integrity than that, even for you."

Lila *did* know, and she cursed the man.

Danny softened. "I *am* sorry. If he liked it here, maybe he'll come back."

She bit her lip. "He did say he worked around here." But the city was large and chances of running into him were slim.

"Let it go." Danny's accent was back, more than likely to distract her, because that was the type of man Lila knew him to be. He didn't like seeing her unhappy. "If it was meant to be, it will be."

She took little comfort in that and brooded through all

the toasts, even after Melanie poked her in the ribs and told her to cheer up.

Buzzing from the champagne, Lila excused herself to the bathroom, just as a group of young men exploded into the bar. Her friends hooted at them before ordering more champagne.

Lila found refuge in the women's lavatory, the quiet soothing after the loud cat-calls. Her friends were in the mood to party, no doubt about that, and the presence of the young men egged them on.

She leaned against the large mirror fastened to the wall. The glass cooled her forehead still feverish from meeting Ben.

His brown eyes, rich mahogany hair, the suit, the stubble, he was every woman's dream. Of course, that was the problem. He was probably married or engaged, but none of that mattered anyway because he'd been able to leave her behind quickly enough.

She used the facilities, cursing her restrictive pantyhose all the while, and glowered unhappily at her reflection as she washed her hands. Her hair was still pinned neatly, the bobby pins poking into her scalp. Her bangs fringed prettily over her forehead, the ends brushing the tips of her eyelashes. Time for a trim. She rubbed her hands under the water using soap that smelled like berries and dried them with soft pink paper napkins. When Danny purchased the bar she'd made him yank out the noisy hand dryers. Women hated them.

She shouldn't have said anything because Danny put her in charge of decorating the entire restroom, an endeavor in which she'd held little interest. But she was proud how it came out. The mauves and beiges were relaxing.

A cabinet stocked with pads, tampons, stomach relief

tablets, condoms, and breath mints was a popular feature that always earned Danny a compliment from his female clientele.

Lila lowered herself onto a mauve loveseat and ran her hands over her cheeks.

Never before had she felt so lonely. True, her last relationship ended a while ago, and true, she had fun being single, but there was something about Ben that made her want to curl into his lap, smooth away the hurt, make him smile, and do it for the rest of her life.

A burst of laughter rang through the restroom door, jarring her peaceful sanctuary. She preferred to be at home.

Then she wouldn't have met Ben. Well, where had that gotten her anyway? Not anywhere she wanted to be. Lila stood, the straps of her sandals biting into her toes.

Determined to forget about a man she would never see again, she pasted a smile on her face, promised herself a good time, and pushed the bathroom door open.

As far as forgetting Ben, this was definitely the way to go. Lila eyed the dark, creepy stone building that sat on the corner of Hamilton and Main and shivered.

Or was that from the cold?

No, it was the club. When Brigid announced she wanted to go to The Maze because "There was no way in hell I will ever step foot in it as a married woman," all her friends agreed at once.

Right before they left The Lucky Clover, Danny had pulled her aside, concerned, and told her to be careful.

Lila had heard stories of The Maze, and she possessed absolutely no desire to party in the club. The stories spanned from deranged to ludicrous, and she didn't know what to believe, nor did she want to find out firsthand.

The warm lobby smelled like cinnamon. A huge bouncer dressed in a black suit jacket skulked in the corner, and the glow of a light fastened to the wall above him bounced off his shiny bald head.

A woman with bright orange hair stood behind a

counter in the corner of the lobby. "Good evening, ladies! Coat check?"

Her boobs strained against the bodice of the black dress, and the neckline looked ready to give at any moment, like a dam about to burst.

Lila handed her jacket to the woman and memorized the number on the ticket she was given in exchange. Four twenty-six. She didn't have anywhere to put the ticket and she resorted to shoving her ID and a twenty into her bra, already regretting leaving her cell phone in the pocket of her coat.

Following her friends—who were chattering excitedly—through the black heavy doors (holy crap she was going to have to start lifting weights—she needed better upper body strength), she stopped abruptly, her foot poised over the floor's metal grating.

Hesitantly, she put her foot down and the sole of her shoe hovered over the tiny rectangles. The heel of her sandal didn't slip through like she thought it would. It felt as if she were stepping onto a cloud, and cautiously she placed all her weight on both feet.

The door closed behind her, trapping her inside the club.

Tentatively, she took a step, then two.

The hostess leaned against a podium, and she too, was dressed all in black. Her blue-black hair gleamed under the lights, and she laughed at Lila's reluctance.

Lila lifted a shoulder self-consciously and stood next to her friends who were looking down onto the dance floor three stories below.

Not ten minutes in, and she already regretted saying she would go along. The thumping music of a Def Leppard song mixed with the champagne from Danny's bar gave her a headache.

God, though, she didn't want to be a party pooper.

Melanie screamed into her ear, "Are you okay?" and Lila nodded, even though she wasn't. She couldn't do anything anyway. She knew The Maze and its motto: "One way in. No way out." They were stuck here until the bar closed, and without her phone she couldn't count down the hours. She was going to have to suck it up, pay her dues for being the maid of honor, and pray her recovery time wouldn't need to be so long she had to call in sick to work Monday.

"Let's go down," Brigid screamed over the music and the group walked around the fourth floor, dodging people drinking, making out, or trying to hold a conversation.

There was nothing to the top floor but the entrance and the hostess. The walls were a glossy black lacquer that reflected the colored lights bouncing around the club from their mounted positions on the beams in the ceiling.

The stairs cushioned her footsteps, and Lila was thankful she wouldn't have any problems walking in her heels. The group huddled to the side of the stairs and began to bicker about what they wanted to do.

Melanie wanted to try the rooms, Brigid, Sasha and Kate wanted to drink and dance. Lila wanted to go home, but given that wasn't an option, chose the next best thing. "I need to find the bathroom."

Brigid rolled her eyes. "Find us on the dance floor," she demanded, taking charge as the bride.

Lila beat a hasty escape. Dancing was going to be as close as she could get to being left alone. There was no way in hell she was going to try any of the rooms. She'd probably walk into an orgy or something.

Oh, sex.

Ben.

She had been doing well not thinking about him, but it hadn't taken much to bring his dark eyes and sexy smile to mind again and dreaming about being in his bed, the rough stubble along his jaw giving her whisker burn in the most delicious places.

Searching for the restrooms, she walked aimlessly, bumping into people as she went. She felt herself up, making sure her driver's license and money were still tucked into her bra, the curved corner of her plastic ID nestled beneath her breast. It brought her back to her college days with Brigid when they would go out on the town, not wanting to fuss with their purses.

She walked past numerous hallways containing the famous, or infamous, doors, and Lila stood at the mouth of one hallway, her fingers restlessly twitching, tempted by the allure of opening one.

Lila hadn't exactly lied to Brigid. She would have to go to the bathroom eventually, she drank a lot of water at The Lucky Clover, but she had wanted to get away from the group. She didn't feel like dancing.

Maybe one door wouldn't hurt. She was curious, and well, when was she ever going to do this again? Brigid forced her to come along. If she'd been in charge of the bachelorette party, like the maid of honor was supposed to be, they would have had a nice dinner out and maybe stayed at The Lucky Clover to drink there. But that would have been too staid for Brigit, and Lila worried how she was going to settle down into married life.

She could barely see the doors, black as they were against the walls, standing out only by the silver knobs on each.

Fuck it.

She was going to try at least one. Maybe, maybe, she would find a way out, and she could use the twenty scratching her boob for the taxi fare. Bolstered by the thought, she stepped around two women making out and steeled herself with the coolness of the knob against her sweaty palm.

Cautiously, she peered around the door, a bright white light surprising her, but crisp cool air made her think yes, she had found a way out. Opening the door wider, the cold air slammed into her face and the sheer drop from a mountain top made her heart plummet to her feet. Sunlight reflecting off the pure white snowy peaks blinded her, and she stumbled backward, pulling the door shut.

Holy shit! Lila flailed backward into the busy hallway, spots dancing before her eyes. She leaned against the wall between two doors and slowly slid to the floor too stunned to stand solidly on her heels.

The sunspots still flashed behind her eyes; she could still smell the clean air. She pressed a hand to her pounding heart, willing herself to stop shaking. If someone would have bumped into her from behind she would have fallen thousands of feet.

She would have died.

The spots subsided and the dark hallway came back into focus.

Everyone was ignoring her.

Good. She felt like a fool.

Lila stood, using the black wall for support.

She abandoned the hallway, all curiosity scared out of her. She didn't want to try another door.

With her mouth dry from fear, Lila scanned the third

floor for a ladies' room. She needed a drink of water and a place to sit for a moment.

She passed a long bar, and a tall skinny man dressed similarly to Danny winked at her and gestured silently, asking if she wanted a drink. She did, but she had a feeling she was going to need to keep her head on straight. She couldn't imagine being drunk and tripping through that door.

"Where's the restroom?" she called over the pounding music, hoping the bartender could hear her.

He pointed to a dark hallway tucked slightly behind the bar she never would have noticed without his direction.

She smiled her thanks, grateful it had been so easy. She found the door with the customary woman's symbol, different from the man's by a skirt and an unflattering hair flip.

Slowly pushing open the door, not knowing what to expect, Lila stepped into the spa of her dreams.

Bright sunlight streamed through enormous skylights, and rock sculptures and huge pots of flowers were scattered on the floor, giving the space a peaceful ambience. The air smelled fresh, like the wind blowing off a prairie, hints of plants and earth in each breath.

She turned a corner and there were rows of massage tables separated by white curtains billowing in a breeze. She didn't know where the wind was coming from, but it wafted the fragrance of the massage oils the therapists were using, rose and lavender and other scents she couldn't name. Women of all shapes, sizes, and colors were on the tables, some on their backs with hot cloths over their eyes, some on their stomachs, and they all looked as if they were in heaven.

One of the therapists caught her watching. "You look tense, hon. You want a massage? I'm almost done here."

Lila was tempted. So tempted to hide in this oasis. To stay and have her hair done (her bangs did need a trim), maybe a facial and a massage. But she'd already been gone too long. This was Brigid's party, and she was the hostess. She was being extremely rude.

Brigid was already frustrated. It wouldn't do their friendship any good to hide until closing time, because she knew without a doubt they were trapped here until then.

Shaking her head, Lila declined, and found the restroom. She had to go now and after she was done she uncomfortably adjusted her pantyhose and dress in the mirror. The last thing she needed was the hem of her skirt caught in the waistband of her nylons. Studying her hair she pushed in some pins that were falling out and tightened the bow at the back of her neck. She grabbed a handful of candy-coated chocolates and dropped them into her mouth, hoping whoever had helped themselves before her had washed their hands.

Lila wandered farther into the spa, wasting time.

She came upon a stone fountain, the young man naked from behind, his smooth buttocks carved from grey rock. The liquid fizzed, and dipping in a finger, Lila tasted the fountain spurted champagne. She circled the fountain. Champagne glasses stacked in a small pyramid, inviting anyone to take a squat glass and fill it to the brim from . . .

. . . The young man's . . . She zeroed in on the statue's body part, and whipping around, she slapped a hand over her eyes.

She wasn't a prude, far from it, but she didn't need to see that.

Women were getting their hair cut, exiting steamy sauna rooms, and even lounging in a huge mud pit.

Her stomach growled; dinner had been a long time ago. She was being a pathetic maid of honor. She ran the first chance she got, then didn't consider food for the rest of their evening. To be fair, she didn't know they would come to The Maze, but maybe there was a place in the club to eat. God knew the place had everything else. A restaurant sure didn't seem out of the realm of possibility. But what kind of restaurant, God only knew.

Lila reluctantly left the spa and went back into the noisy hallway of the club. The tranquil sound of a harp was cut off sharply by music from Evanescence.

She gave the bartender another smile of thanks. She was about to ask him if there was a restaurant in the club so she could report back to Brigid—if she was hungry, her friends probably were too—when a man in a black tuxedo approached her, the white of his dress shirt purple in the black light.

His long blond hair was pulled into a ponytail and his ears glittered with diamond studs. From his pocket peeked a hot pink pocket square that matched his hot pink cummerbund.

He looked like a cheesy extra from an eighties wedding movie, and Lila smothered a smile.

He bent low to speak into her ear. "Allow me to escort you to your group."

Ah, Brigid must have sent in the troops. She wasn't surprised. Brigid would be President one day. No one got away with anything with her around.

"What's the password?" Lila yelled back, teasing him. While she and her friends were growing up, they always had a password for everything. They came up with something all of them would know and understand: the science teacher's name they all crushed on, the color of the evil lunch lady's shirt, and always, always, Danny's name because even when they were kids, he'd been gorgeous. As time went on, their passwords became more grown up: favorite wine, Beau's name from *Days of Our Lives*, creepy bosses.

She was tricking Mr. Tuxedo, but no matter. It would be safer to let him take her down to the dance floor than to try to find it on her own.

"Four twenty-six," he said close to her ear, his breath hinting of peppermint mouthwash.

Lila blinked in surprise. Undoubtedly he was staff if he knew her coat check ticket number. Reassured, she put her hand in the crook of his elbow when he offered it.

Mr. Tuxedo led her through the throng of partiers. The club was packed, people waiting three deep at the bars dispersed throughout the third floor. Half the city must have been in The Maze tonight.

A magician took residence in an alcove off to the side of the throughway near the stairs leading down to the second floor, and Lila tugged on Mr. Tuxedo's arm, urging him to pause. They stood for a moment and watched the magician pull a fat white rabbit out of a black top hat. Lila was about to continue on when the rabbit, in a puff of smoke, turned into a sleek black and white zebra looking ludicrous in a matching black top hat.

"Oh, that isn't right," the magician lamented into a microphone attached to his lapel to the crowd sitting on a small set of bleachers.

The audience clapped at the trick and laughed at the magician's dismay.

"Zebra! What are you doing here?" the magician scolded to the crowd's delight.

The magician aimed his white-tipped black wand at the zebra. "Get out of here and go back to the zoo where you belong."

In a white puff of smoke, the zebra disappeared.

A blonde woman with a Victoria's Secret model's figure took the zebra's place. Naked, but for white bunny ears and white high heels, she stared at the hollering crowd, covered her breasts, and ran off, disappearing quickly down one of the hallways with black doors.

"Come back!" the magician hollered, flinging his hands into the air.

The audience roared and the magician bowed to wild applause.

"He's good," Lila shouted to Mr. Tuxedo, who patiently waited while she watched the show.

"That's my Uncle Sandy," he told her, leaning toward her to be heard over the music and the applause of the audience. "He got me the job here."

"What do you do?"

Mr. Tuxedo tugged on her arm and he led her down the stairs to the second floor.

It seemed more of the same to Lila: more partiers, more bars. A cigarette girl in a white and silver dress sauntered by, a black tray held in place by a strap around her neck, test tubes full of bright liquid on display.

Mr. Tuxedo escorted her to a hallway spotted with people lounging on loveseats, settees, and benches, drinking or making out. Two women and a man were leaning over a mirrored plate full of white powdered lines. Lila had never seen drugs in person. She didn't travel in those social circles, and she gave them a wide berth, appalled at what they were doing in the open.

Black door after black door lined the black hallway, making Lila's head spin. The hallway appeared the same as the others and was never-ending.

"I thought my friends were on the dance floor?" Lila asked, growing uncomfortable.

He flashed her a reassuring smile.

Just when she didn't think the hallway would stop, they reached the end, a door with a silver knob stopping them.

Lila wasn't surprised her friends had tried a room, and she was curious what was behind the door that captivated her friends so thoroughly they didn't want to leave to find her.

Unless they couldn't leave.

Lila met Mr. Tuxedo's eyes. In the darkness of the club she couldn't see what color his eyes were, but here in the hallway, in the glow of light drifting from a crystal chandelier, they glittered brown, revealing none of the warmth of Ben's eyes at The Lucky Clover.

He grasped the silver knob.

"You know what?" Lila swallowed. "I've changed my mind. I think I'll go—"

Before she could finish, the man grabbed her upper arm. "Remember when you asked me what I do here?"

Lila nodded before she could stop herself.

Mr. Tuxedo opened the door. "You don't want to know."

He pushed her into the room.

CHAPTER THREE

L ila flailed in the air, the darkness enveloping her. She felt as if she were in one of her dreams, the ones where she fell from a building or from a plane. When she woke from those dreams, her heart pounded, she was drenched in sweat, and her legs were tangled in the damp sheets.

She hoped this was the case now, hoped she would wake up in her bed, her cat lying next to her, the familiar feel of her fuzzy blanket beneath her fingers.

But the cold air felt too real, the pull of gravity too strong.

She landed on the hard ground, her head slamming onto a rock.

The drop knocked the breath out of her, and she struggled to inhale, pain running up and down her spine, her head throbbing from the impact of the fall.

It took several minutes, but once she could breathe, she sat up, holding a hand to her head as the room spun.

Only . . . it wasn't a room. She was outside.

She was outside!

The excitement of the discovery she was free of The Maze faded. She didn't have her jacket and she was already shivering.

A bird squawked, his call setting off a string of replies.

Lila rubbed her hands up and down her arms.

Tall evergreen trees and other trees she couldn't identify loomed above her blocking out the moonlight.

A man dressed in camo fatigues and brown boots jumped out from behind a tree, a rifle clutched in his hands.

"We've been looking for you everywhere," he growled softly, kneeling next to her.

"*You have?*" Lila asked.

"Where the hell have you been?" he asked.

"How about dropping from the sky," she retorted, her back still hurting from the fall.

This information didn't even make him blink. "Are you okay?"

"No, no I'm not, thanks for asking. I'm cold and hungry. And what do you mean, 'we've been looking for you'? Who's we? And why were you looking for me?"

"Whoa, lady, one question at a time." He pulled a grey and green backpack from his shoulders. "I can help you out. Here." He pulled a crackling silver packet from his pack and unfolded the little rectangle. "My name is Devlin; you can call me Dev." He shook out the blanket and even in the dark it shimmered.

Lila warmed slightly when Dev draped it around her shoulders. "Thanks."

Dev sat on the ground, relaxing from his kneeling position. "You said you're hungry?"

"Yeah."

Dev went back to digging through his backpack. "I would use a light but we can't let them find us."

"Them?" Lila wasn't getting the full story, but she wasn't sure she wanted it. Fricken messed up club. "Listen, where's the club from here? I need to get back. I have friends waiting for me."

"No can-do. Here. My mom makes me protein bars made out of peanut butter and chocolate." He held it out to her then pulled it back. "You're not allergic to peanuts are you?" His eyes were earnest, his voice full of concern.

At least someone decent found her, because if she would have been found by a wack-job like Mr. Tuxedo, she would have been shit outta luck, as her mother liked to say.

"No, not peanuts. Broccoli, though. Which came in handy when I was a kid."

Dev laughed. "I bet it did. Here." He handed her the bar and rooted around for something else.

Lila unwrapped the bar as fast as she could. Even with the tin foil blanket she was chilled and her fingertips were numb. So was her butt.

She took a bite and her mouth filled with gooey peanut butter and chocolate. She moaned in ecstasy and forgot how cold she was. "Oh my God," she mumbled around the mouthful. "These are amazing."

Dev grinned. "I know. She makes them for me when I work out. The secret ingredient is the grasshoppers. She buys them online and grinds them up into the finest powder in her food processor. Perfect protein."

Lila fought back the sudden churning in her stomach and the strong desire to vomit. Ground up grasshoppers? Holy shit.

Dev pulled a dark green Thermos out of his bag. "Thirsty?"

She was, but like hell if she wanted to drink some weird goat milk smoothie or something.

"What do you have?" she asked warily as she rewrapped the bar in the plastic wrap and casually hid it in the grass behind her. There was no way freaking way she would eat the rest. She would starve before she would eat the rest. She didn't care how much peanut butter and chocolate was in it. Lila felt guilty for littering but it couldn't be helped.

"A double chocolate skinny cappuccino with no foam." He smiled winningly. "From Starbucks." Dev poured some into the tin cup cover of the Thermos.

The drink seemed innocent enough, and the chocolate scent of the steam smelled delicious. "Thanks," she said, reaching out for the cup.

It tasted fine and the sweet liquid warmed her as it slid down her throat.

"I don't mean to rush you, but we need to get going."

"Can you help me get back to the club?" Lila asked again.

"Nope." Dev said, standing. "We've been looking for you and I need to get you back to base."

"Base?" Lila parroted.

"Yep. We have to keep you away from Team Black. We can't let them win, the bastards."

"What do I have to do with this?" Lila was confused.

"You're the prize." Dev spoke to her as if she hadn't been listening. "We're the Camo team. We keep you away from Team Black. If they steal you, we could lose and no one wants to lose."

Dev took the tin cup from Lila, screwed it back onto the Thermos, and shoved it into his backpack. He slung it over his shoulder. "Let's move out!"

Let's move out? Was he crazy?

"I'm not walking anywhere. I'm cold and I want to go

back to The Maze. My friends are probably wondering where I am." She tugged the blanket tighter around her. At least she didn't feel sick anymore, but her back still hurt.

Before Dev could respond, gunfire filled the air.

"Lady, they're getting closer. We need to get going."

Her choices were few. She could make a run for it, but her survival in the middle of the woods was slim to none—and that was only if she made it away from Dev in the first place. The man was huge and his grasshopper muscles bulged. It was obvious he could outrun her.

"Where's base?" she asked, resigned. Maybe there was a cabin not far from here with a fire. She was glad she went pee when she had the chance. There was no way she was going to screw around with her pantyhose while she was squatting behind a tree.

"Quite a ways from here, actually. It will take a while to make it back. That could be good for us. Staying in one spot makes it easier for them."

"Fine." Lila's voice was clipped. She was *so* not happy about this. Losing Ben, turning down a massage, and eating grasshopper hadn't made this night into anything Lila wanted to repeat.

Her heels sunk into the top layer of the ground when she stood. She followed Dev, trying to stay on her toes. Branches, shrubs, tree roots, and grass made walking difficult, and Dev had to wait several times for her to catch up.

"Can't you move faster?"

"You try walking in these." Lila lifted a foot to show him her heels.

"Take 'em off," Dev commanded, hands on his hips. His dog tags moved in time with his impatient huffs.

"Are you out of your mind?" While taking off the heels did indeed sound like the best idea of the decade, she wouldn't be able to walk without them. "How would I make it anywhere? We're in the middle of the woods in case you missed it."

Again, gunfire echoed through the quiet night.

"We need to keep moving." Dev dry washed his face in irritation. He secured the blanket around her shoulders and threw her over his, her head brushing the side of his enormous backpack.

"Hey!"

Dev pulled off her sandals and dropped them to the ground.

"You can't carry me like this," Lila protested. "And those are Manolos."

"Lady, I don't give a shit what those are, and you don't weigh more than a hundred pounds. I carried my buddy through ten miles of ninety degree heat in Afghanistan to find him medical attention after an IED exploded. I could carry you like this for the rest of my life."

Lila grappled with the blanket before it slid to the ground. Being in Dev's arms helped, his hand warm on her thigh where he steadied her.

But there was no tenderness in his touch. Nothing that indicated she was anything more than a prize in this game he had to win. He was all business.

"Thank you for doing that." Lila felt silly. She'd never thanked a soldier for his service before.

"No need to thank me," Dev said gruffly. His boots were snapping twigs and branches as he walked them to God-knew-where.

Lila hoped he knew where he was going. "I'm sure your friend appreciated it." It seemed odd carrying on a conversation, her voice drifting down to what she supposed was a very fine ass.

What? She wasn't dead.

She was more than a bit put out Dev had thrown her shoes. He could've carried her with her shoes on and she wouldn't be out the six hundred dollars she'd spent on the lovely pair of Manolo Blahniks.

Men.

"He didn't make it." Dev's voice was soft, barely louder than the wind blowing through the bare trees.

"Oh. I'm sorry." Lila lost a friend in high school to a drunk driver, but she knew it wasn't the same.

"Shit happens."

Dev didn't say any more than that.

Pressed into Dev's hard shoulder, Lila's ribs started to hurt. She tried to prop herself up on his backpack the best she could, but it didn't help much.

Dev's strong strides never faltered, not even when he had to skirt a massive tree that had fallen.

"Do you know where you're going?" Lila finally asked. Between the blanket and Dev's body heat she was warm enough, but her feet were cold and tipped upside down was making her faintly nauseated. Though, in all fairness, that could have been the grasshopper bar.

Dev didn't answer.

Occasionally, the faint popping of gunshots made gooseflesh travel up and down her arms. She wondered how Dev was handling the noise. He had seemed happy-go-lucky when he'd found her but now was focused on getting to base and nothing else.

Water gurgled over the wind and the crunching noise Dev made with his boots, and Lila prayed a lake or river would make them stop.

She didn't feel in danger per se, but she wasn't entirely comfortable with the situation either, pushed through a door and landing in the middle of some godforsaken woods. She could let herself panic over how she would get out of here and back home, but Dev was in the same situation. He had known about The Maze, so maybe he had chosen poorly and ended up here as well.

He put her down.

Rocks and grass poked the bottoms of Lila's feet, but it could have been worse.

All this could have been worse.

A lot worse.

Hansel and Gretel and crazy old woman worse.

They stopped at the bank of a black shallow river. A wooden bridge crossed it, and large rocks jutted from the water. If she'd been wearing her running shoes, she could have tried to jump across.

She shivered under the blanket. Her stomach growled and she hoped Dev didn't hear it. Thankfully, he'd forgotten about the protein bar.

"You can stretch," Dev told her. "Base isn't that far away now. Do you want more cappuccino?"

"No, thanks. Let's keep going." She wanted to get where they were going as quickly as possible.

Dev had one foot on the ground and one foot on the wooden bridge when a voice shouted from below.

"Halt! No one crosses my bridge without my permission." A squat man with a barrel chest crawled up the bank from underneath the bridge. His face was lumpy like a potato, his hair a bright red exploding around his head. He was dressed in burlap pants, a dark brown from what Lila could see, a light brown shirt and a dark leather vest. A belt encircled his waist, hammers and machetes of all sizes wedged into the loops.

He was even shorter than Lila's five foot one inch frame,

only as tall as her shoulders. The man scowled, crossing his arms over his massive chest.

"What do you mean, we can't cross?" Dev demanded. "I just came this way. I need to get this prize back to base."

"Hey!" Lila objected. She wouldn't let herself be demeaned and belittled. She was more than a prize in a stupid game. She was a person and she'd be damned if she let Dev forget that.

Dev had the courtesy to look chagrined. "Sorry," he muttered.

Lila accepted it. She'd better because she had a sneaking suspicion that was all she was going to get.

"No one's crossing my bridge," the man insisted grumpily. "Unless . . . you can answer my riddle."

"A riddle?" A bridge. A riddle. A squat old man. "You're a troll!" Lila announced.

"Don't be stupid," Dev scolded, agitated. "He's just an old man Team Black sent to slow us down. Move out of the way and let us cross."

Lila hugged the blanket around her. It was a good blanket. Big. It pooled around her feet, keeping her bare legs warm. It even warmed her feet a little though the bottoms were cold from the ground.

"Dev, he's not going to let us go over his bridge until we can answer his riddle," she tried to reason with him. "Don't you remember the fairy tales?" Lila did, and she knew it was unwise to make trolls mad.

"Oh, yeah, yeah." He snapped his fingers. "My little brother was watching *Dora the Explorer* and Map sent Dora over a toll bridge, but it wasn't a *toll* bridge, it was a *troll* bridge. Boots helped her answer the riddle."

Lila blinked. "You watch *Dora the Explorer*?"

"My little brother is three. My mom's on her second marriage."

"Oh." That wasn't any of Lila's business. "Okay. Anyway—"

"Can we get on with it?" the troll cut in grumpily. "You interrupted my nap."

"What's your name?"

The troll scowled. "What does that have to do with the price of milk in China?"

"About forty-nine Yuan Renminbi," Dev supplied immediately.

When Lila gaped, Dev shrugged. "What? I went to see the Great Wall of China a couple years ago. I still have friends there."

Lila was losing her grip. "Fine. Whatever. Can we get on with it?"

"Good idea," the troll agreed, glaring at both of them. "Are you ready for the riddle?"

"Come on old man. Let's get this done." Dev slipped his backpack off his shoulders and sat on the ground. He drummed his fingers impatiently on his knees.

Lila leaned against the bridge's handrail and skimmed her toes against the wooden planks. She wasn't worried about the rocks and slivers making holes in her hose. They were heavy-duty. They had to be, to keep her flab sucked in.

The no-name smugly looked at them. "What's my address?"

"What? How in the hell are we supposed to know that? I don't even know where we are."

Lila's throat closed and she had trouble breathing. She squeezed her eyes shut and tried not to cry.

The night was beginning to weight on her, and she missed Ben. She'd let him slip right through her fingers and it was her own damn fault. At least, if she had made a move, she would have found out if he was taken and she could have said she'd tried. But now, not knowing, it would always eat her up inside.

"Yeah, man," Dev agreed. "I was at The Maze with my friends on leave and we tried this room. We thought it was paintball until we realized it wasn't." A shadow passed over his face.

"You have friends out there?" Lila asked.

"Yeah. We're all military home on leave. We thought the club would be a great way to blow off some steam."

Lila felt sorry for him, and she was about to tell him so when the troll whined, "Come on. It's an easy question."

"What is this river anyway?" It would give her a clue to where she was. The whole thing seemed surreal. Maybe she would wake up and she'd find out she dreamed the entire thing. She hadn't dreamt Ben, though. If she concentrated she could feel the stubble on his jaw, see the sadness in his eyes.

"This is the Lillibrooke River," the troll told them, shifting from foot to foot, tugging irritably on his long red beard that matched his hair.

Well, that ruled out half the United States, but it didn't help much. Lila went through all she knew about the river which was basically nothing. "Are we still in Cedar Ridge?"

The troll shrugged.

"We're a ways out of town," Dev noted, "if we're even still in the area."

"You grew up here?" Lila asked.

Dev nodded. "Yeah."

"What do you remember about the river? Anything from school?"

Dev shook his head.

This was getting them nowhere.

The troll's address. The troll's address.

He lived under this bridge. A smaller bridge that crossed the Lillibrooke River. Why was there even a bridge? For hikers? Were they in the state park?

She asked Dev.

"I camped in the park a long time ago but none of this looks familiar."

Lila rolled her eyes. "But you think the park is where we could be."

"Lady, I don't know. We could be anywhere."

"Stop that. My name is Lila." She rested her head against the supporting rail of the bridge. A silver plaque she hadn't noticed before caught some of her hair and she tugged her strands free from the rough corner. "Do you have a lighter in your pack?"

Dev dug in his backpack and brought her a small box of matches. He lit one of the little sticks, and the flame flickered in the breeze. He shielded it with his other hand so it wouldn't blow out.

Lila ran her hand over the plaque.

DEDICATED TO TREVOR CALHOUNE
FUR TRADER, EXPLORER
DISCOVERER OF THE LILLIBROOKE RIVER 1804

The troll waited impatiently, pacing back and forth, the tools of his belt rustling against his rough pants. His boots crunched the cold ground.

The sound made Lila shiver and she pulled the blanket closer around her.

Back to the task at hand. What made up an address? A house number, a street name, a city and ZIP code. If she were to make up an address based on what she knew, she had the state. Maybe. Possibly the street name if she used the name of the river. She couldn't guess though, until she had a number.

Trevor Calhoun discovered the area in 1804, probably trekking all over the place like Lewis and Clark.

"Are you sure you don't know anything about the river?"

Dev blew out the match before it burnt his fingers and shoved the little box into one of the huge pockets of his fatigues. "No. Huh uh. We went to the conservation building in middle school. Did you do that? We walked around and the guide told us about the area and the river. One of my classmates, Jeremy, was goofing around and he fell in, the asswipe. The guide had to jump in and swim him back to shore. He got a month's worth of detention."

Lila had gone to the conservation building in middle school, too. They'd learned lots of little facts about the river. How wide it was, how long.

How long.

And then it clicked.

"That was really good thinking," Dev congratulated her sometime later. "I have no idea how you came up with it. I would've been stuck there for the rest of my life. Goddamn troll."

Lila was slung over Dev's shoulder again. He'd assured her they were on the right path and would reach base any minute.

She didn't know what path he was talking about. There was no path, only sticks, trees, burrs and rocks. "It kind of came to me. You helped, bringing up the conservation story. My class went there too and somehow I remembered the river facts."

The Lillibrooke River's length.

Four hundred and twenty-six miles from source to mouth.

426 Lillibrooke.

That was all the troll wanted, and he let them pass.

But not before giving Lila a cold congratulatory bottle of Sangria. Apparently she was one of few who was able to solve the riddle.

Lila had only gotten a sip of the frosty wine before Dev impatiently took the bottle and rammed the cap back on. He didn't want to waste time standing around drinking. Being that they could have been standing there for the rest of the night if the troll wouldn't have let them by, Lila thought she earned it, but she didn't say anything.

Dev hadn't given her the chance anyway. The minute he fastened his backpack, he had thrown it, and her, over his shoulder and they'd been on their way.

Dev stepped into a grassy clearing and a cheer rose up among the men pacing back and forth, agitated and bored. A different group of men wearing black huddled together, and a few men wearing camouflage held rifles near them.

He dumped her on the ground near a huge bonfire, and she watched him accept high fives and slaps on the back. For capturing her, she guessed.

Lila tucked the blanket around her, disgusted. This game was stupid. And it scared her a little. Those guns looked real.

She was no prize. Or her ex-boyfriend wouldn't have treated her like she was a cheating piece of trash.

Ben wouldn't treat her that way.

Oh, stop it, she told herself, holding her hands out to the fire, inching as close as she dared. Dammit, it was cold out here. *Stop feeling sorry for yourself.* She had a great life. A good job, good friends.

Danny.

So what if she didn't have a man? She had a cat. Who probably expected her home by now.

Dev sat next to her and handed her another tin cup of cappuccino. She accepted it gratefully and was almost comfortable with the blanket and fire.

After she gave the cup back, Dev said, "I'm sorry, Lila,

but I'm going to have to tie you up and blindfold you. We can't take a chance that you'll try to run away. This game is important."

Lila snorted. There was nothing more important than getting the hell out of here. "What will you win?"

Not that she cared, but she didn't like the way he was digging into his backpack.

He wasn't looking for more grasshopper bars.

"You. You knew that."

Lila's blood ran cold. "What do you mean?"

Dev pulled strips of black cloth from his pack. "When we win, someone gets to keep you."

"You are out of your mind!" Lila exclaimed, her stomach sinking with fear.

"No, no. It's not like that," Dev assured her, smoothing the strip of cloth over her eyes and tying the knot behind her head. Dev pulled loose a couple of the bobby pins holding her updo in place and her hair spilled down her back and along her cheeks.

"Then what is it like?" Not being able to see scared the crap out of her.

"Drinks, maybe. I don't know."

Like hell she would. She didn't care if they served their country or not. She wasn't a hooker.

Her resolve solidified when Dev bound her hands behind her back. He had to pull the blanket off her and the cold air mixed with the heat of the fire on her skin.

She flexed her hands, bitter.

How in the hell was she going to get out of this mess?

Lila didn't know how long she sat there. Sometimes Dev kept her company, sometimes he left her alone, and when he did she could hear his voice carry over the clearing and the crackling of the fire.

She felt sorry for Team Black, huddled together like scared hostages. She hadn't gotten a good look at the group; she only knew this game must have been going on for a while because there were a lot of captives.

An acrid smell floated through the air and she wrinkled her nose in distaste. It smelled like the gross smoke bombs some idiot brought to a baby shower luncheon at the country club a few months ago. Simon something. The idiot's brother and wife were having a baby and Lila was friends with the mother-to-be. Simon and his brother thought it would be hilarious to reveal the sex of the baby with colored smoke bombs. That didn't go over so well.

Imagine that.

A shrill shriek sounded and a scuffle started. A fight had broken out. Maybe the Team Black members finally retaliating.

She wished she could see. She could stand and try to run, but with her hands behind her she couldn't take her blindfold off. With the luck she was having tonight she would run straight into the middle of the trouble, not away from it.

While deciding if it was better to stay put or maybe try to creep away, a rustling near the ground caught her attention and she cocked her head to listen. Someone was approaching. "Who's there? What's happening?" Maybe Dev had come back for her.

"I'm going to get you out of here . . . Lila."

The man's voice sounded familiar, yet she couldn't place it. He tried to loosen the knot at the back of her head, but Dev had tied it too tightly. He gave up and started on the binding on her hands.

"You know who I am? Are you playing the game?"

He knew her name. She'd only told Dev and she didn't

think he would have bothered to tell anyone, if he even remembered it. She was the prize, not a real person. He hadn't introduced her, and besides cheering for her capture, the Camos hadn't given her one glance.

The man chuckled. "No."

He freed her arms and she cried out, the pins and needles pricking her skin as blood rushed to her hands. She must have been sitting for longer than she thought.

"Shh. It's okay. I know you must be freezing."

He rubbed her arms for a moment, and his palms felt good against her skin. Not only the warmth, but the touch. It made her heart beat faster. Awareness pooled in her belly, and his familiarity—

Her thought was cut off by him wrapping his jacket around her. It held his body heat and it enveloped her, the woodsy scent of his cologne fighting with the bitter smell of the smoke bombs. He hugged her to him and she melted into his embrace.

"I want to get you away from here, but you have to trust me, okay? I'll take off your blindfold when we have more time. I don't want to get caught."

His voice was gravelly yet smooth, pitched low, his mouth near her ear so she could hear over the sounds of the scuffle.

"You sound familiar." His identity was just out of reach, slipping through the fog in her memory that was as thick as the smoke filling the clearing.

It was getting hard to breathe.

"Are you okay? How are you feeling? Are you cold?"

"I'm hungry. Thirsty. I had a blanket until not long ago. I don't know what they did with it." She was warming up with the man's jacket though, and she concentrated on the smell of his cologne.

"At least that was something," he muttered.

Easily, he picked her up, and Lila snuggled into his arms and rested her head against his shoulder. She felt safe. She trusted him to get her away from this stupid game. Maybe he could get her back to The Maze. After all, he had to have come from somewhere himself and maybe he wanted to get back to the club too.

He walked them away from bonfire, and she was relieved and surprised no one tried to stop them.

The smell of the smoke bombs dissipated, and the yells, screams, and gunshots faded.

They walked for a long time, and she almost fell asleep with his sure steps through the brush, the warmth of his jacket, and being cradled in his arms.

He stopped and sank to the ground, keeping her in his lap. Lila didn't mind. She felt safer in his arms than she had with Dev. Dev had been friendly enough, but he'd tied her up, and not in a good way. Oh, God, she shouldn't be thinking about something like that at a time like this. No, Dev had gotten an edge to him when he'd joined his friends.

She was glad to be away from them.

"Who are you? Why did you save me? Didn't you want to win the game?"

None of the Camos had given her a second glance after Dev had brought her into the clearing; they hadn't been inclined to help her one little bit. The guys in black hadn't been able to help themselves, much less her.

Lila felt him work on the blindfold.

"I did. I have the prize, don't I?"

She laughed, not thinking of it that way. She supposed he had won the game, but what would Dev and his friends do after they realized she was missing?

He pulled the blindfold away from her eyes and she got her first look at her savior. "Ben."

Ben. He was here. He was here, and she was in his lap, and he had rescued her. She pushed her face into his chest and tried with all her strength not to cry. He pulled her closer and she wrapped her arms around him. Praise God she'd gotten another chance.

"How in the hell did you get out here?"

Lila heard the concern, and hope saturated her heart. *No, no, Lila. Play it cool.* She'd gotten a miraculous second chance and she couldn't waste it.

"Where are all your friends?"

She couldn't bring herself to pull away so she spoke into his shirt. "When we got to The Maze, we were separated almost right away. I had to go to the bathroom, and the others went to get drinks and dance. After I was done in the bathroom, a guy in a tux—I thought he worked at the club—told me he would help me find them. Instead he led me down a hallway and pushed me through a door, and, I don't know how, but I fell into the woods. Before I could look for help to get back to the club, I was taken hostage in the game. It could have been worse, I guess."

Hell yeah, it could have been. Dev had been kind with his grasshopper bars, and she was thankful he had waited until they reached base before falling off his rocker.

"Getting warmer?" Ben asked.

"Yeah. I'm lucky you didn't check your jacket. Thanks." She hoped he wasn't cold. It was as freezing as downtown.

"I didn't plan on being in The Maze for long. I got a call from one of my friends saying they needed help and this address. I've never been here before and I'll never come back here again."

She laughed. She agreed with him one hundred

percent. Damn Brigid for wanting to come to the stupid club. Yet . . . how could she be mad at her friend now? Ben would have been lost to her forever, but he was here and she was in his lap with his arms tight around her.

"Lila," Ben said urgently, pulling away. "Where's Danny? Shouldn't you have called him for help?"

"I left my phone in my jacket. My dress doesn't have pockets, and I hate shoving it in my bra."

Which was true. Her driver's license and the twenty were enough, the smooth plastic of her ID not bothering her. But her iPhone was a large bulky thing and her industrial strength case made the phone cumbersome.

"Won't he be worried you haven't gotten home yet? My phone was stolen, or I would check the time and call him for you."

He probably wasn't home yet anyway, so it wouldn't matter if she called him.

"We don't live together. He won't know what time I get back." Thank God for that! She didn't need to live with him. He was a slob of the highest order and it drove her mad. She wasn't immaculate by any means, but, no, she didn't want to live with Danny.

"We should probably keep moving. We need to find a way back."

Or, I could stay here forever, she thought, content, as Ben started to rub his hand down her leg to her foot. Her feet were cold, but nothing she wasn't used to, having to wear sandals and heels every winter.

"It seems impossible."

She sounded sad, but it wasn't because of the thought of *not* finding their way back. It was the thought of *finding* their way back. She didn't want to go back, not now, after finding Ben.

Going back meant back to her lonely life, her stupid life, of watching her friends get married and have babies, while her boyfriends followed her around like puppies and turned into suspicious jerks.

"Have you ever been to The Maze before?" Ben asked. He tucked her body into his and Lila vowed to remember every second for the rest of her life.

"No. Brigid wanted to try it. I didn't want to. I thought we were going to other bars downtown. I changed my mind after we went in though. The hallways and doors, the dance floor, the levels. It was all so spectacular. Even going to the bathroom was amazing. I just wanted to go pee but there was a spa inside. You could stay for any kind of treatment: facial, massage, a woman was even getting her hair cut. It was baffling and marvelous all at the same time."

Ben shook his head and his chin grazed the top of her head, his whiskers snagging her hair. "The Maze isn't all fun and games. I watched Cy shoot someone and he looked dead. Dead-dead. If you know what I mean."

Yeah, Lila knew what Ben meant. Dev's rifle looked plenty real to her, too. "Who's Cy?"

"He was on Team Black and helped me find base. He was the one with the smoke bombs. I left him behind with my other friends."

"I hope they'll be okay." There had been a lot of gunfire and smoke in the clearing when they snuck away. A stray bullet could kill in an instant.

"They'll take care of each other. We all want the same thing."

"To go home," she whispered, but she liked where she was. Yeah, it was cold outside, but she was oh so warm inside now. Ben had found her. He'd found her, and rescued her, and now he was holding her, and oh God. Her heart was in her throat, and she didn't know what she was going to do.

"I'll help you get there. I promise."

There was a little moonlight shining between the clouds and the trees and it glittered in his espresso-colored eyes.

"Thank you." *What was that?* she berated herself. *No. No, thank you. Don't thank him for taking you home and dropping you off at your stupid lonely apartment with no one around but the cat.*

He stood, and she gripped his shoulders.

"You should put me down. You can't walk through these woods carrying me the whole time." She wiggled in his arms, but it made him tighten his grip. I could get used to this. *Too bad*, her internal voice kept up the monologue. *He belongs to someone and you know it. It's why he left your ass in Danny's bar. He's only being nice.*

Ben's voice broke through her depressing thoughts. "There's no way you can walk without shoes, and you wouldn't have made it far in high heels anyway, so say 'thank you, Ben' and enjoy the ride."

Lila knew it was true. She had tried to stumble around, and it took Dev mere seconds before growing too frustrated to let her walk on her own. "I guess you're right," Lila agreed with him, "but I don't want to be a burden, and it's not your job to take care of me."

She wanted it to be though. She wanted to be able to call him if she needed help. She wanted to be able to lean on him for love, comfort, peace.

And more than anything, she wanted him to need her because she wanted be there for him.

He didn't say anything.

He probably agreed with you, dummy, Lila fought with herself, and he didn't want to say it out loud.

Well, fuck it. Her mother always told her, if you don't ask, the answer is always no. So, fuck it.

"I missed you at the bar. I said something to Melanie and when I looked back, you were gone."

"I only stopped for a drink after working late. I didn't mean to stay for so long."

Well, there was a rebuff if she ever heard one. But she wasn't done, dammit. She opened her mouth to say something else then stopped. Maybe she shouldn't press him. He was under enough pressure. She didn't know how he ended up in the woods. He said he answered a friend's call for help, but she didn't know which friend, or if he'd managed to help at all. He might have had friends at that stupid base.

The Maze was huge; his friends could have been anywhere.

They walked through silence thicker than the ham and pea soup her mom liked to make. It was just as gross.

"You might as well say it."

So he knew she wasn't done. Lila blew out a laugh. Part of it was surprise, part of it relief. Her laugh was louder than she intended and she clamped a hand over her mouth. "Do you think it's okay if we make noise?"

Ben stopped and listened.

Lila strained to hear too, but there was nothing but the hoot of an owl, and the rustling of dried leaves, made maybe by a squirrel, possibly a chipmunk.

She held her breath, waiting.

Hefting her in his arms, he broke the silence. "I don't hear anything. I don't think anyone is after us."

"Is that good?" She bit her lip. "That's good, right? Or not good? Should someone be looking for us?" Lila didn't know what the hell to think. She didn't want Dev chasing them. On the other hand, she didn't like feeling they were all alone out here. And it did feel as if they were in the middle of nowhere.

Ben hugged her closer. He was strong; she could feel the muscles in his arms along her back and under her knees.

"I wouldn't mind seeing my friends," he said, "but with the way the Camos were playing, I wouldn't want them looking for us. They didn't hurt you, did they?"

Lila pressed her cheek against the smooth lapel of his suit jacket. "No. They blindfolded me when we got to base, and tied me up, but the leader was very nice. He might have taken the game a little too seriously, though." Dev *had* been nice. Up until he had tied her up and offered her as a sacrifice.

"They all were," Ben said, snorting his disgust.

Might as well go for broke. He knew she had more to say anyway, so she might as well just do it. Even if she didn't have her Nikes on. "I was going to say . . ."

He took her a few more feet and she pulled away the best she could so she could speak to him, rather than to the bare trees and the black night. As she did, he looked down at her. She thought she would be looking at his chin, at his jaw, maybe up his nose, but God, he stared at her and his eyes bore holes into her soul.

He whispered, "What?"

Lila wished he would lean down and kiss her. Unable to stop herself, she lifted a hand to his cheek. "You seemed sad, at the bar."

Ben didn't answer and kept moving.

Great job, Lila. His rigid jaw told her he didn't want to talk about it. His silence confirmed it.

Ben tripped and she squealed, hanging onto his neck so he wouldn't drop her.

"What the hell was that?" Ben growled.

She tried to look through the dying grass and sticks but she couldn't see anything.

Ben started kicking around, and his toe came in contact with something solid. He kicked at it, following it along. "This is an old train track," he said surprised.

Lila was lost. "What does that mean?"

"It means—"

Lila waited.

"I'm not sure," he admitted after a few moments. "These tracks haven't been used in a long time. I was thinking if we followed them . . . but if they haven't been in use, I don't know what we would find, or how long it would take to find it."

"A better plan than nothing."

It sounded good to her. At least, better than freaking wandering around the woods. She didn't want to be bothering Ben any more than she was. He was surly, probably freezing, and even if he was refusing to put her down, his arms had to hurt.

"You think I didn't have a plan?" he teased.

"You should put me down. I can walk."

"I'm not putting you down. The ground is covered with sticks and rocks, and you're cold." He paused. "Follow or not follow?"

He was asking her? What did she know? Asking her was like flipping a coin: heads you lose, tales you lose. But what the hell? It's not like a poorly made decision on her part would get them into any more trouble. "Follow."

"East or west?"

West might put them back at base. She didn't want that. Ben's friends might be nice but the last she saw, they weren't helping anyone. "Ummm, east."

Ben followed the track. She didn't know how he could

see it under the brush and bracken. Maybe he felt the ties under his shoes.

"What are you thinking?" he asked.

She needed to get her mind off their situation.

"Just wishing I knew where we were." Well, that didn't help.

"I won't hurt you. I would never hurt you, Lila. I swear."

Right now, in these woods, in The Maze, she wouldn't trust anyone more than she trusted Ben. She didn't know why except she remembered the pain in his eyes. If he knew pain, he wouldn't hurt her. "I know. When you disappeared from the bar, I didn't think I would ever see you again. You paid in cash—there was no way for me to find you."

Probably he hadn't wanted her to find him. Too bad that didn't work out.

When he didn't say anything she felt like a fool. They walked out from a group of trees and a huge train tunnel yawned at them. She didn't think a train tunnel would help them much and she was about to suggest they turn around when he asked, "What do you think?"

Lila thought they were in a shit-ton of trouble, if she was being honest. She shrugged. "This seems hopeless, either way."

Ben didn't turn around, instead carrying her deep into the tunnel.

She was glad she wasn't scared of the dark. If it had been a phobia, she could easily picture herself having an anxiety attack.

Ben carefully lowered them both to the ground.

Lila scrambled out of his lap. She didn't want to cause any more trouble for him than she already had. He was probably cursing the moment he found her, but his gentlemanly ways wouldn't allow her to go without rescue.

She drew her legs up under the jacket and with the tunnel keeping out the elements, she was almost warm.

Lila couldn't see a thing and she gasped in surprise when she felt his arms around her. What was he doing? Did he want to kiss her? She felt his hand reach for the pocket of his jacket. Oh. He was digging for something.

"Sorry," he muttered. "Do you want a sip?"

A sip of what? Well, whatever. He carried something. Maybe if she got drunk she could fall asleep until morning.

"It wasn't you," she assured him. "I mean, it was you, but you surprised me, that's all."

"Don't worry about it." Ben patted down her arms and found her hands pulled up into the sleeves of his jacket. His hands were cold on hers. She felt a little guilty for taking his jacket, but she couldn't offer to give it back. She would freeze without it.

He pushed a cold metal flask into her hands and unscrewed the cap.

Lila took a sip and fought off the cough that always followed the liquid fire.

She felt for his hands and carefully gave it back. She didn't know if he took a sip for himself or not. She couldn't see and he was being very quiet. "Thanks."

He didn't respond, but he passed the flask back to her. With the wine the troll had given her, and now with what she guessed was whiskey, Lila felt queasy. She took a small sip and was about to hand it back when he spoke.

"I *was* sad."

She paused for only a second before she leaned into him. She wanted to comfort him because the pain she saw on his face at Danny's bar, she could now hear in his voice.

Ben wrapped an arm around her and it gave her courage. "What happened?"

"I told Danny. He didn't tell you?"

She shook her head. No, he hadn't, not that she hadn't tried her damnedest to find out.

"A few weeks ago my fiancée left me for another man," he said bleakly. "She'd been seeing him behind my back. I was stewing about it, I guess."

Sympathy oozed for him. No wonder he was so skittish. Lila took small comfort it wasn't her. Well, maybe not all her. "Oh. I'm sorry." And she was, for the woman. She couldn't imagine being stupid enough to let him go.

She handed him the flask; she didn't want any more.

He screwed the cap back on and set it down. It clanked on the track when it fell over. "It was for the best. We didn't love each other. She was just the one who admitted it first."

Lila was relieved he was free. Maybe she had a chance. "Still though. It's hard when a relationship ends. How long were you together?" Oh, that sounded nosy. She rushed on, "You don't have to answer that. It's too personal. Sorry."

"No, it's all right. It wasn't too long, actually. But to me it felt right. We were comfortable, never fought. Agreed on everything that mattered. It was like . . . living with my sister, or a friend. We had a camaraderie. Recently I was told that's not how I should have felt about her and that's why she left. To find passion. She found someone else and left," Ben said, hugging her and brushing a kiss against her forehead.

Oh God, she was in trouble. Being this close to him, his lips on her skin, made her dizzy.

"She found what she was looking for and I've let her go. We're still friends. She left me her cat."

That idea seemed so absurd she giggled. Cheat on your fiancé with another man and then ask him to keep your cat.

He was a very kind, considerate man to not harbor any ill will towards his ex-fiancée.

"How about you? How long have you and Danny been together?"

Lila's heart skittered to a stop. She and Danny? How did he get an idea like that? His name caught in her throat. "Danny?"

"Yeah," Ben said, and Lila couldn't pinpoint all the feelings behind that one word. Resignation? Sadness? Disappointment? "You two seem close, and I saw how much he loves you. You guys are lucky. I want that, one day."

"I am lucky." She was extremely lucky Danny was in her life. She didn't know what she would do without him. "But so's his wife."

Which was true. He treated Mollie very well, and he loved her very much. Lila had been scared, at first, she was losing a brother, but she'd gained a sister. She loved Mollie too, and she adored her little niece.

Ben pulled away. "He's having an affair with you?" he asked, sounding horrified.

Lila laughed, and the sound echoed off the rock walls. Danny having an affair was as likely as her ever visiting The Maze again. Never in a million years. "No," she said firmly. "Danny's my brother."

"So who is the lucky man?" Ben asked immediately.

"No one. My last relationship ended a while ago and I've been enjoying being single, waiting for the right man to come along."

She'd been enjoying being single, all right. Her relationship with Logan had been a nightmare. It finally took Danny and the threat of a baseball bat to leave her alone.

She took Ben's hand. "I met you in the bar and I was

thinking maybe . . . but you seemed so sad, and when you up and left, I thought maybe it was for the best."

"That's what I thought, too. I thought you were with Danny and it was the right thing for me to do. To go. I didn't want to though."

She squeezed her eyes shut and made little sparkles burst behind her eyelids. Hearing his low voice confess he hadn't wanted to leave her behind made her skin prickle and sweat washed over her skin along with . . . desire.

She was alone with Ben in the dark and he'd confessed he wanted her. Kind of. How long had it been since she'd had sex? And not with herself, thankyouverymuch.

He hadn't wanted to leave her, he was single. He knew now, she was single too. There was nothing stopping them, so she ran her fingers up his chest, over his tie, her fingers skimming over his tie clip.

She cupped his face, her fingers grazing his whiskers.

Lila's nose bumped his and she was glad he couldn't see her cheeks flame, but he laughed and adjusted his head so their lips met. He tasted of the whiskey they'd been sipping, his scruff rubbing her lips and cheeks.

"Are you all right?" he asked.

"Yeah. This isn't so bad after all." Putting aside the fact they were in the middle of nowhere and she was hungry and tired.

She wanted to kiss him again so she leaned toward him, inviting him to make the move this time, but he pulled away from her.

"What was that?"

Lila listened, but there was nothing. The tunnel was quiet, except for the pounding of her heart and the echo of their breathing made louder by the absolute silence. "I don't hear anything."

"Listen."

A low, thin whistle sounded in the distance, and in the next second a train followed the curve in the track, blinding her with its light. "What's happening?"

"The train." Ben pulled her to her feet and the rocks bit into the soles. "There's a train on the tracks."

"I don't understand." She ran after him, the rotting wood and rocks gouging into the bottoms of her feet. She stubbed her big toe and she bit the inside of her cheek to keep from crying.

He stopped running to face her. "We're in the train's tunnel and there is no space for us to get out of the way. Do you get it now?"

No, she didn't get it now. The tracks were abandoned, even she saw that while they were following them. Why a train now? It had to be some kind of sick joke.

They were too far into the tunnel to run.

Ben must have realized it too for all he did was wrap his arms around her and say, "I didn't think it would end like this."

Who thought about how they were going to die? Maybe she did, every once in a while, but being run down by a train certainly hadn't been on her list of ways to kick the bucket.

Especially now since she may have found the love of her life.

In the engine's bright light, Lila memorized Ben's face. She would take this night, these delicious few hours with him, knowing he wanted her, over a lifetime of not having him. "I was happy to have found you, for a little while."

Lila had never spoken truer words in her life. She hid her face in his shirt, breathing in the scent of smoke bombs.

She tensed, waiting for the impact.

Ben's embrace was like chains wrapped around her, but

it was no match for the tornado-like winds that pulled her from his grasp.

His name died on her lips, the pummeling air, ironically, taking her breath away.

She didn't know which end was up as she was spun around like a sock in the spin cycle of a washing machine.

As quickly as it started, it stopped.

The smell of popcorn and peanuts slammed her senses after the clean air of the forest.

Lila took a moment to get her bearings, her stomach doing somersaults, her eyes squeezed shut against the violent wind that stopped as quickly as it had started.

She lay flat on her back, her head resting against something solid. She tried to move but she was pinned, though she could still turn her head left and right.

Gingerly, she opened her eyes and immediately bit back a horrified scream.

The biggest, ugliest creature was standing next to her head. It had a transparent, bulbous body, little arms, long legs, and feelers protruding from its face.

Lila, with the bright spotlight glaring on them, saw through its body to the creature's pulsating fluids. A brownish-red, it looked like a crab, a crayfish, a lobster, and its giant mouth was turned in a ghastly, joyous smile.

It wore a top hat, a black bow tie, and the thing held a saw in its . . . claw.

Its eyes were positioned on either side of its head and in one shiny black circle she saw herself lying in a long rectangular box, her bare feet jutting from the end, her head protruding from the other side.

She swallowed another scream. This creature was going to saw her in half.

Lila tore her eyes away from the bug, and in the other

direction there was a sea of them, more of the insects, sitting in bleachers watching a human climb into a big black cannon.

With a sinking realization Lila identified the creature who was now steadily sawing into the box in which she lay.

It wasn't a crab, or a lobster, or even a crayfish. It wasn't a bedbug or a tick.

It was a flea.

Lila was trapped in a flea circus.

CHAPTER FIVE

The saw's teeth tugged at Ben's jacket and she finally allowed herself to scream.

The flea miraculously pushed apart the two halves of the box.

Lila's feet stuck out the bottom, but she swore they were still attached to her.

There was a chittering sound, perhaps the fleas clapping their little claws.

The flea bowed, pulling his black top hat from the curve of its head, and when it pointed at Lila, the applause grew louder.

After the chittering died down, the flea pushed the two halves together. She didn't feel any different, but she was grateful when the flea lifted the top.

The spotlight shifted and plunged them into semi-darkness, which was just as well, because the flea creeped her out.

How the hell was she going to get out of this, and where in the hell was Ben? Oh God, where was he? Lila prayed with all her strength he was okay.

With a thunderous boom, the human man blew out of the cannon landing into the center of a huge net.

Once again, the tent was filled with chittering at the trick.

The man climbed out of the net by a rope ladder, then a flea attached something sparkling around his neck. The insect led the human away, and the spotlight switched to a woman with long blonde hair sitting on a trapeze swing.

The flea that had sawed her in half poked her and lifted a gold rope tied around her neck.

The cord was fine and smooth; she hadn't felt it until he tugged at it, pulling her.

Unwillingly, she followed, stumbling in her haste.

The rope tightened around her neck warning her to keep moving, and she followed the giant bug, its feet scratching the cement floor.

Bile rose in her throat. That thing was disgusting, and it made her feel dirty.

Ben's jacket flapped around her legs, and she tucked her hands into the sleeves to hide her fists. She couldn't tolerate much more of this, but there were so many of them in the stands. She didn't know how she would escape.

The flea pushed her toward a ladder and gestured with a shiny claw to climb up to a tightrope that was suspended hundreds of feet in the air.

Lila panicked. She was deathly afraid of heights. There was no way in hell this insect could make her climb that ladder.

Unless it tightened the rope around her neck, cutting off her air supply.

Alrighty then.

It nudged her again and she swore there was a menacing look in the thing's eyes.

It would kill her if she didn't comply.

With shaking hands, she climbed the ladder. The top was almost to the tent's ceiling. She was going to die. She would never see Danny again. She wouldn't see her niece grow up. She would never see Ben again. She wouldn't have any of her own children.

Wait. Did Ben want kids?

To keep her mind off the ground that was getting farther and farther way, she focused on Dev and the smoke bomb war, and she hoped all of Ben's friends made it out of the woods, out of The Maze. Maybe they were all in stupid, screwed up rooms like she was.

That was small consolation. She wouldn't wish this on anybody.

Hopefully Brigid, Melanie, and the rest of her friends stayed out of the rooms, that they only danced and drank, but Lila knew the allure of The Maze was overwhelming. Even she had wanted to explore after swearing to herself she wouldn't.

Lila was half way up the pole, climbing in the semi-darkness, because the spotlight was shining on another act. A human man was standing on the back of a zebra, little fleas sitting near the ring. Lila paused on the ladder and looked for the lady on the trapeze, but her act ended. The swing was empty and her ring was dark.

She kept climbing, the flea below staring up at her to prevent her descent.

Drenched in sweat, she reached the top. There was a small platform attached to the pole and she stood on it, clinging to the red metal pole with all her strength.

The spotlight blinked on her and she squinted against the glare. Apparently that was her cue, and it was evident what she was supposed to do.

She wouldn't be able to get to the other side without falling. The tightrope, which wasn't a rope at all, but a metal cable, seemed a million miles long and too thin to walk on.

Lila sniffed the collar of Ben's jacket. The woodsy scent mixed with the smoke bomb stink calmed her and she took a tentative step onto the tightrope. Instinctively, she held out her arms for balance before placing her other foot in front of the first.

To her surprise, another human started to meet her from the other side. This human was a male and the way he held himself seemed vaguely familiar.

As they inched toward each other, Lila fought the urge to hurry, to push the bastard off the rope.

"Logan Henrickson," Lila hissed in disgust. "You son of a bitch."

"Lila." He sighed her name in obvious relief. "Thank Jesus Christ. We gotta get out of here."

"You mean, *I* need to get out of here. You can rot here for all I care."

"Don't be like that," Logan begged. "I've changed."

Lila pushed the hair out of her face. She swayed on the rope as fury blinded her and she started shaking from head to foot in rage.

But she didn't fall.

"You've changed because Danny threatened to splatter your brains all over the sidewalk outside my apartment building when he caught you stalking me."

The atmosphere of the circus shifted; no longer was there a feeling of joy and anticipation for the next act. Expectation filled the air, a hunger, and several fleas waited below the tightrope staring at them, pointing.

"We need to get out of here," Logan repeated uneasily, tugging Ben's jacket.

"What's going on?" Lila whispered. Her gaze darted around the circus tent, but she couldn't see any immediate threat. She could only sense it.

"Let's go." Logan pulled on her arm.

Following Logan, who also had a golden rope around his neck, she trailed behind him on the tightrope and carefully lowered herself onto the rope ladder.

When Lila glanced down, fleas and humans alike were waiting for them at the bottom.

Her knees were knocking together with nerves, and when her feet were planted firmly on the ground, her vision tilted as her equilibrium returned. She didn't know how she survived.

Among the humans, Lila recognized the blonde trapeze artist and the man who had been blown out of the cannon. They were waiting in the group with the fleas, their "handlers" making sure they didn't escape by holding onto the golden leashes around their necks.

Logan protectively put his arm around her, and she let him. Something wasn't right and she needed all the support she could get. She wished Ben was here and she hoped he was faring better than she.

"What's going on?" Logan asked the man, trying to sound brave.

The blonde and the man Logan addressed were both wearing one-piece black leotards.

Lila wanted to ask the blonde how long she had been trapped here that she wasn't wearing her street clothes anymore. She was about to open her mouth when the man answered Logan.

"Feeding time."

Lila woke, her body on fire. She felt like she had when she was little and had inadvertently bothered a hornet's nest. She was lucky she wasn't allergic to their stings, her pediatrician told her mother, or she would have died. She'd had hundreds of stings all over her body, and that was the way she felt now. Stinging, sore, achy. Maybe she even had a fever.

"Are you okay?"

Logan's voice cut through her misery, and she slowly opened her eyes. She was lying in a large room full of cots, each occupied by a human attached to some kind of IV drip.

She swallowed thickly, her mouth and throat dry. "What happened?"

"Those sumbitches had us for a snack, that's what happened."

Lila searched for the source of the voice. There were several more humans in here than she'd seen in the ring. The voice came from behind her but she couldn't see unless she sat up, and she was too tired and sore to do that.

"Are you slaves?" she asked.

The guy snorted. "Yeah. I don't even know how long we've been here. We can't get out."

That was unacceptable.

She needed to get out. To find Ben. She needed to see he was all right. She needed to see that he hadn't been a dream.

"Fuck that."

Logan still wore his street clothes. Maybe that meant he hadn't been here as long as the others. He was propped up in his bed, the same fluid bag as everyone else's attached to his wrist by a piece of tape.

She agreed with Logan, which was almost as possible as finding the eighth wonder of the world. "Right. Fuck that."

But she would fuck that later. Right now all she wanted to do was sleep, so she did.

"It wasn't you, you know."

Logan's voice irritated her. She was tired, goddamn it. He needed to leave her alone.

Her eyes popped open.

The fleas.

They needed to get the hell away from the fleas.

Thankfully, she didn't feel so achy after her nap and she found the strength to sit.

Peeling the tape off her IV and yanking the needle out of her vein, she glared at Logan. "We should be thinking of a way out of here, not rehashing the past." Lila chewed on her bottom lip. "You were in The Maze?"

"We all were."

It was the same voice, the one coming from behind her. He had blond hair and bright blue eyes. His complexion was a chalky white, and his figure too lanky. "Do you know what day it is? What year?"

Gaping, Lila scrambled for the date. "It's December fifteenth, 2015," she supplied. "I'm Lila."

"Stephen. Thank God. I was sure I lost years being here."

"Did you?" asked Logan.

Stephen shook his head. "No. That's the night we went to The Maze—"

"You have others with you? Here?" Lila hoped to God Ben wasn't here. "Have you seen a man with dark brown hair and eyes, wearing a black suit?"

"No. Was he with you?"

"Kind of." That was the best she could do. They hadn't come to The Maze together and they wouldn't leave together, either, but she shouldn't be thinking about that now. All these people needed out and no one seemed inclined to try. Stephen sounded damned bleak.

"We need to get out of here." And goddammit she was tired of saying it. She was ready to do something about it.

Logan pulled his IV out of his wrist, splattering blood on the cot.

Lila glared. "You're still a son of a bitch. No offense to your mom. She's a really nice lady."

"I told you, I've changed. Lila, I'm sorry."

"Ah huh." Lila shook the arm of a woman lying on a cot next to her. "We're getting out of here."

The woman's eyes opened into little slits. "For real?"

Gently Lila peeled the tape back from the woman's dark skin and pulled the IV out of her arm. "For real."

Wonder, amazement, and hope floated across the woman's pinched face.

"Spread the word, help who needs it. We're getting out and we'll do it together." Lila brushed her bangs out of her eyes.

"I got help and I'm engaged now."

Lila whirled, but before a scathing word left her mouth, his earnest, sincere face softened her.

His black hair was shiny under the sickly green fluorescent lights of the warehouse, his green eyes blurry from lack of sleep. He towered over her, his t-shirt from the latest rock concert rumpled, his jeans showcasing his rock-hard thighs.

She'd always had a thing for tall, dark, and handsome.

"Good for you," she muttered.

Hope floated through the air as word spread there was

possible salvation. People were helping each other, and they were looking to her.

Lila rather felt she was like Katniss Everdeen, sent to free all of mankind.

She lifted her chin.

Call her Lila Donahue: Hummingbird.

That made her smile even though she had never been more scared. Not even the time she'd gone on the roller-coaster at Six Flags and puked her guts out afterward.

She deferred to Stephen since he seemed to think he'd been there a while. "Is there a doorway? An exit? Maybe not back into the circus tent."

He pointed to a beige door on the far end of the ware-house. "I've seen them come and go from there. I think it's the only door in the place, but whenever I'm in here, I'm always a little bit out of it."

If it was the only door, it was the only option. She hoped the hundred or so people here wouldn't panic and cooperate with her.

"Stephen, tell them the plan, keep them calm," she instructed.

"This is a new side of you," Logan noticed, impressed.

It was. And she liked it.

"You know, it wasn't what you did, I knew you wouldn't hurt me, but you made me feel as if I wasn't fit for anybody, that nobody could ever trust me. Do you know how degrading that is?"

Far across the warehouse people were ripping the IVs out of their arms, standing from their cots, and congregating at the door. Some of them were weak, and they were stumbling. The woman who'd been sleeping next to Lila, and Stephen, were helping to pull out IVs and keep everyone focused.

"I told you, it was me, not you. I was so fucking afraid you were going to leave me. You're perfect. So goddamn perfect. I didn't deserve you, I knew I didn't. I couldn't wrap my head around the fact you were mine. I wanted to keep you, and I went insane with it because I knew you didn't love me back."

This was all news to Lila. Logan's stalking, his needing to know where she was at every turn, his calling her at work to affirm she was there, it had all been demeaning and it had made her feel untrustworthy and stupid.

"Well," she bit out, "you're right about two things. I never loved you and you didn't deserve me." She paused, watched the people wait near the door. "I would've liked to watch Danny beat your head in."

Logan winced. "So harsh."

"Let's g—"

Just as she was about to take a step toward the door, two fleas came out of the shadows.

Stephen must not have known about the other entrance, but it was too late to be angry about it.

"Run!" Logan yelled.

Lila didn't need to be told twice. Her stockinged feet slid across the buffed floor. She slipped and Logan righted her, grabbing onto her elbow.

"Whose jacket is this, anyway?" he grumbled, huffing.

Lila forgot she was wearing Ben's coat. She was so comfortable and warm, she almost said, "Mine."

"Do we need to go into that now?" she asked, exasperated, as the two fleas chittered and scraped their way toward them.

"Just making conversation," Logan joked, keeping hold of her upper arm.

The people crowding around the door made way for them.

"There's a keypad and card slot," Stephen barked at them. "This was a horrible idea." He frowned at Lila, blaming her for the approaching fleas and the punishment they would dole out for trying to escape.

She rested her head against the door's cold metal. Card slot and passcode, card slot and passcode.

Lila still believed she was Katniss, sent to save the world, or at least, the slaves in this horrific flea circus. Although, this was The Maze, and being enslaved was definitely not real. So the way to get out of here wasn't real either.

"Logan, do you have your driver's license with you?"

"No! Are you crazy? What would that do?"

The fleas were gaining on them.

"Okay, okay." Maybe it was a dumb idea, but it was all she had. Lila fished in her bra for hers and rammed it into the slot.

Passcode.

People were mumbling, a few of the women started crying. One young man broke from the group and ran away, but it did not keep the fleas from coming at them.

"What's your coat check number?"

"What the fuck, Lila? I don't remember. I threw the ticket away."

All looks and no brains was Danny's description of Logan. There, she had taken umbrage, feeling Danny was mocking her choice in men.

Now she completely agreed.

"How did you expect to retrieve your jacket then, you idiot?"

"What the fuck?" Stephen burst out. "Did you two used to date or something?"

"Or something," Lila muttered.

Passcode. What the hell? She didn't know. With shaking fingers she punched in her social security number. The little red light in the upper right-hand corner blinked at her.

Nope.

Ummm, what else? What else could freaking mean anything? She tried her employee identification code.

Nope.

Her old school bus number.

Her birthdate.

"Lila!" Logan growled.

"Well, you tell me what number to use!" Lila cried, her hands shaking wildly above the keypad.

The fleas were close. Too close.

"What was *your* coat check number, Miss High and Mighty?"

Of course.

Lila steadied her right hand, her left hand bracing her wrist, and punched in a four, a two, and a six.

The little light blinked green, the door buzzed.

"Go, go, go!" Stephen shouted pulling the door open and running through first.

Quite the gentleman, Lila thought bitterly. *I bet you would have been the first on a lifeboat when the Titanic sank too.*

Logan helped herd the flea circus slaves through the door.

Many stopped to thank Lila or kiss her cheek for helping them.

Through her fear as the two fleas approached, angrily squeaking at them, Lila felt a burst of pride.

It took many long seconds for all of them to run through the door. Not one of them hesitated even though no one knew where the hallway would lead.

When the last person went through, the fleas were shrieking in protest and were nearly upon Logan and Lila.

"Thanks, Lila. You're a lifesaver." Logan disappeared.

One of the fleas reached out to grab her, but she stepped through the door. She felt its claw clutch at the material of Ben's jacket before it slammed shut behind her.

CHAPTER SIX

She ran down the dark tunnel, blue auxiliary lights along the ceiling showing her the way. Logan hadn't waited for her, or The Maze had taken him somewhere else; she didn't see his shadow in front of her or hear his footfalls.

Abandoned, Lila swallowed back a lump of fear. She felt very alone, but it was a substantial upgrade to being trapped by the fleas.

She slowed, her heart pounding.

Her feet were damp, the concrete wet, shallow puddles dotting the floor. Pipes ran near the ceiling. Any more of this and she was going to develop a phobia.

The tunnel curved slightly, and a white light up ahead made her run faster, Ben's jacket slipping around her shoulders.

The light shone from beneath a door at the end of the tunnel. Without a second's hesitation, she pushed it open, and she stepped into what looked like a recreational room.

Tables and chairs decorated the space. Couches, loveseats, and bookshelves sat on gleaming white tiled floors.

Potted plants and flowers made the room cheerful with brilliant spots of color. A giant flat screen TV attached to one wall played C-SPAN with a meeting on mute, and on screen a little white dog ran around on the brown carpeted floor playing hide and seek among desks and people's feet.

With no immediate threat apparent, Lila shook out her shoulders and rolled her head to relieve the tension in her neck. An ache had started behind her eyes.

A group of elderly people filed into the room, and an older Black woman wearing light green scrubs pushed a black utility cart into the room, a silver mesh cage sitting on top.

With red-painted lips, the woman smiled at her. "You here for Bingo chile?" she asked in a thick Southern accent. "It's twenty dollars fo' four cards."

No, she wasn't her for Bingo, wherever *here* was, and she opened her mouth to decline and politely ask for a way out when a small woman in butter yellow pajamas and a blue chenille robe shuffled into the room, talking animatedly with another older woman wearing pink and white striped tights, a pink tutu, and a pink t-shirt that announced she loved to dance.

The woman's odd ensemble didn't faze her. She focused on the woman in the blue robe. It couldn't be. It just couldn't be.

"Grandma Jean!" The words burst out of her mouth before she could stop them. Even though the older woman couldn't possibly be her grandmother.

Her Grandma Jean had been dead for going on ten years.

The woman smiled brightly and held out her arms. "Lila!"

She didn't resist. She ran across the room dodging

chairs, tables, and people taking their places for the Bingo game.

"Oh, Grandma!" Lila cried as her grandmother enveloped her with strong, scrawny arms.

Her grandma was as short as she was and she comfortably rested her head on her grandma's bony shoulder.

Grandma Jean nudged her back and said, "Come on now, we don't want to be holding up the game."

The Black woman, whose name was Mabel according to the white nametag pinned to her green scrubs, stopped them. "Jean, you know guests hafta pay. No sneakin' her in, even if she is as cute as a button."

"I don't have my wallet," Jean complained, her arm around Lila's shoulder.

"I can pay, Grandma," Lila said, regretting the words immediately. She didn't have any money.

"It's twenty dollars," Mabel reminded her.

Oh. Twenty dollars. She *did* have that tucked into her bra. She reached into the side of her dress, and pulled the twenty from the underside of her boob.

Mabel took the bill between her thumb and forefinger, grimacing in distaste, but handed her four cards, the typical BINGO letters printed along the top, the grid of numbers in the center. Mabel also handed her a neon-pink colored dauber.

Lila sighed happily, blinking into her grandma's faded brown eyes. She loved playing Bingo with her grandma.

"Leona is my friend," Jean introduced them, walking along the uneven aisles created by the white tables pushed around the room.

The three of them sat at an empty card table, and Lila sat as close to her grandmother as she could.

One of her first memories was sitting in her grandma's

lap playing Patty Cake, her grandma's soft voice singing the accompanying song about the baker man.

She wanted, with all her heart, to climb into her grandmother's lap, but Lila would bet her four Bingo cards she weighed more than her grandma now.

"What is this place? Is Grandpa Charlie with you?"

"Of course he is, dear, but you know he hates Bingo. He's getting a lap dance down the hall."

Lila choked on her own spit. "W-what?"

"That hussy," Leona grumbled, laying out her cards.

"But doesn't Grandpa live with you?" Lila almost dropped her cards onto the floor and she put them on the table along with the dauber.

She rubbed her eyes. Her dauber was shaped like a penis.

"Are you crazy, dear? The less I see of that man, the better. I put up with him for over sixty years. If he can still get it up, then so much the better with another woman."

Her grandma had always seemed happily married up until breast cancer took her life. Her grandfather followed her Grandma Jean soon after.

Lila had always believed it was because he missed her grandma so much. Now, apparently, it was because he wanted lap dances from hussies in the afterlife.

Mabel thumped the palm of her hand on the microphone and said, "Y'all can hear me? Make sure you can hear me. I won't tolerate no pissin' and moanin' because y'all have your hearing aids off and Lester is the only one who can hear." She fluffed her grey hair.

Lila's Bingo cards were filled with fours, twos, and sixes. There would be no way she could win.

Her grandma's brown eyes were shrewdly scanning her

cards, daubing each number Mabel called out with an aqua blue penis dauber.

Leona's "fuck" every time Mabel called a number she didn't have aside, Lila was in heaven and she wondered if this was her grandmother's idea of heaven. Bingo with a friend while her husband was ... ah ... entertained.

Lila wanted to pour her heart out as she had in the past. Boyfriends, friends, clothes, first job, homework, she complained about it all. Some things never changed.

After sitting through the game, Lila soaking in her grandmother's presence, she followed her grandma down a beige carpeted hallway.

"Fucking Lester," Leona muttered, trailing behind them. "Always gotta fucking win."

Grandma Jean winked at her. "Lester always wins. He gets it on with Mabel, and she makes him take her to the Denny's on buy-one-get-one free days with the money he wins."

"Don't make it right."

"I'm going to take Lila to my room for a cup of coffee. Why don't you go play backgammon with that young man you're always playing with? What's his name? Heath something?"

"Don't remember his last name. Something to do with bookkeeping." Leona smoothed her tutu and straightened her t-shirt. "I hope I'm dressed all right."

Grandma Jean rolled her eyes, and Leona turned around, grumbling as she shuffled away.

Lila grabbed her grandma's hand, happy to have her alone.

They walked by a door held open with a black and white cat statue.

"Oh, look, there's your grandpa. Say hello, honey."

She peeked around the white multipurpose door, equally excited to see her grandpa. Her grandfather, dressed in grey dress slacks, a grey and black striped dress shirt, and an unbuttoned black cardigan, dressed in Heaven as he had on earth, and Lila knew without a doubt his breath would smell like peppermint.

A woman older than the hills gyrated on her grandpa's lap wearing nothing but a bright pink lipstick smile and a blonde wig that inched off her head with every wiggle. Gravity had not been kind, and uneasily, Lila patted her own breasts. "Oof," she said, backing away.

Unfortunately, watching her late grandfather enjoy a lap dance wasn't the strangest thing she'd seen tonight.

"It's all right, dear," Grandma Jean assured her. "Better her than me. Here we are," her grandmother announced as the hallway dissolved and they were standing in the home her grandma and grandpa had lived in all their lives.

Danny, Mollie, and their daughter lived there now.

Lila fought tears, the familiar kitchen bringing back many wonderful memories. Her grandmother had collected cows and the little figures lined the countertops and window sill.

The homey scene and the constant scents of coffee and chocolate chip cookies soothed her. Weary from the night's events, Lila sank into a chair at the table.

She'd spent many hours doing homework, eating cookies, and drinking milk at this table. She ran her fingers along the bottom finding the gobs of bubble gum she'd sneakily stick there, too lazy after school to throw it away.

Grandma Jean set a plate of chocolate chip cookies and a mug of coffee in front of her, prepared her coffee exactly how she liked it: half coffee, half milk. Her grandmother drank it that way too.

Her tears dripped off her chin making a puddle on the blue and white speckled Formica tabletop.

"Oh, darling," her grandma murmured, stroking Lila's messy hair. "What is it, dear?"

She didn't know where to begin.

"Clothes, boys, or homework?"

Lila laughed and wiped her cheeks, then picked up a cookie. It was bright pink, like her Bingo dauber. She put the cookie back on the plate; maybe it wasn't a good idea to eat anything in this dream.

And it was a dream. It was the only way Grandma Jean could be alive.

"Boys, I guess," she said, twisting her fingers together in her lap.

"You make such poor choices," her grandmother clucked at her.

"I know!" Lila wailed.

Grandma Jean took a sip of her coffee. "What are you looking for?"

Lila immediately thought of Ben. The golden warmth of his eyes, the way he held her, his soft kiss.

"Someone to love me," she whispered.

"Oh, Lila," Jean scolded, slamming her coffee mug onto the table, making the light brown liquid slosh over the side. "Haven't you learned anything by now?"

Her grandma's disapproval made her bristle. "What do you mean?"

"It's not who will love you, but who will you love? Lila, sweetheart, all my life, and in this afterlife too, you've dated men who worshipped you, kissed your feet, gave you whatever you wanted, whenever you wanted it. You're pretty, and smart, yet you have no respect for yourself, or others."

"What about Logan?"

"He wanted to give you everything and was damned upset when you decided you didn't want it. He tried to hold on to you, but you never wanted him. Lila, you want a dog, you go to the shelter and adopt a dog."

Lila bowed her head in shame.

She was nothing but a spoiled little brat. She'd demanded everything from Logan, and when she got it, she didn't want it anymore.

He hadn't needed to change. He'd gone back to his normal self after they broke up. She'd been the one to fuck him up.

"You choose men who want to give you the world. But what do you want to give them in return?"

From the moment she had looked into Ben's eyes, she had wanted to take his pain away. She hadn't one thought about herself, only what she could do for him.

What a unique concept.

"Ben is the first in a long string of beaus who didn't fall at your feet."

"He left me at the bar," Lila whimpered.

"No sweetheart," her grandma corrected her gently. "He taught you good people are worth the fight. He wants to give you the world, that's true, but he'll make you work for it, and it's what you need. You may not like it at times, but you'll respect him more than you've ever respected another man."

Logan was wrong. She wasn't perfect; she was a selfish bitch.

Ben walked away from her, but Fate had given them a second chance. Fate gave *her* a second chance. She wouldn't waste it.

Grandma Jean softened her eyes, and brushed Lila's hair away from her face. "Come on, let's go sit in the living room for a small rest. Everything will seem better after a nap."

It was what her grandma always told her. Things always did seem better after some sleep.

She followed her grandma to the same faded blue reupholstered couch she remembered from her childhood.

Grandma Jean sat at one end and Lila sat in the middle, bringing her feet up, and laying her head on her grandma's lap.

She pulled Ben's jacket around her and with her grandma humming "Patty Cake," Lila fell asleep.

CHAPTER SEVEN

"Miss? Your makeup is done. Miss? Wake up now. We're set to begin filming in fifteen minutes."

Lila's eyes slowly opened.

"Miss?"

A woman holding makeup brushes and a makeup compact jiggled her shoulder.

"I'm awake."

"Don't smear your make up. It took forever to do while you were sleeping and there's no time to redo it."

Lila's reflection met her eyes in the huge mirror brightened by a long row of lightbulbs along the top.

Bright red lipstick coated her lips, and huge blush circles colored her cheeks. Electric blue eyeshadow sparkled on her eyelids and her eyebrows were drawn in more heavily than she had ever done them.

She looked ridiculous.

"They want you on set," the makeup artist told her, shoving the brushes into a wide drawer. A white mouse poked its head out, wiggling its little pink nose, his ears twitching. His paws rested on the lip of the drawer.

Weird.

"Ah, okay?" Lila still reeled from seeing her grandma. She missed her grandparents so much, and spending time with grandma, playing Bingo, made the feeling increase tenfold in her heart.

"No crying either!" the lady snapped. "They think I can work a miracle whenever I feel like it. No one understands the skill and talent it takes to make mediocre people ready for TV."

"Hey!" She looked silly, but that wasn't her fault. The lady at the Clinique counter in Bloomingdale's said she had beautiful coloring, great skin, and fantastic bone structure, thankyouverymuch.

She followed the makeup artist down a brightly lit hallway and she paused to glance at the framed photos that lined the cream-colored walls. In one, she stood, standing next to . . . who was that, the purple mouse from Chuck E. Cheese's? In another she was smiling, and . . . holy fuck, the Pillsbury Dough Boy had his arm around her.

"Come on. If we're late, it's my fault."

Lila scampered to catch up with the makeup lady, her skinny behind twitching in a faded pair of jeans that fit her like a second skin.

The hallway spit them out onto a TV set decorated for a talk show.

A tall grey padded stool sat on a dais, with two of the same padded stools flanking it. A large screen hung from the ceiling behind the stools and on the white background pink goofy letters spelled out "The Lila Donahue Show."

She had her own talk show.

Sweet.

Oh, no, no. That wasn't sweet.

She had stage fright like crazy, and she hadn't been on a

stage since Kindergarten when she froze up playing a sunflower, and her one line, "I'm a sunflower!" had never been uttered.

The experience ruined the stage for her, forever.

"Places!" yelled a man dressed in blue jeans and a white dress shirt. He wore a headset with a microphone positioned in front of his mouth and waved a clipboard at her in greeting.

Hundreds of people murmuring with excitement filed in and took their places in the audience chairs.

Holy shit, her show was popular!

"Places!" the man barked at her.

What did he want her to do?

"Sit down," the makeup artist clarified, grabbing Lila's shoulder through Ben's thick jacket and pulling her toward one of the grey stools.

Lila hoisted herself onto the middle stool and placed her feet on the foot rest. Her feet were filthy from running down the tunnel fleeing the fleas.

Haha.

Lame, Lila. Lame.

"Quiet on set!" the producer, or whatever his title was, yelled, and thrust cards into her hands.

Oh good, she wouldn't be going in blind.

Before she had a chance to look at her cards, music began and a voice boomed over the speakers. "Welcome to the Lila Donahue Show!"

Lila straightened in the chair and pasted a smile on her face. The audience stared at her and started to clap.

"And now for today's guests," the announcer continued after the applauding stopped, "Mr. and Mrs. Claus!"

The audience burst into welcoming applause and cheers.

Lila scanned them as they clapped. They looked like normal, every day people.

A tall man and a shorter woman walked onto set, stage left. He was dressed as Santa, with the red and white hat, wire rimmed glasses, and white beard. He wore the familiar red and white velvet jacket with the black belt and golden buckle, matching red pants, and black boots.

Mrs. Claus wore a similar red and white hat, the same wire rimmed glasses as her husband's perched on her little nose, her cheeks as a bright pink as Lila's. She was dressed in a red velvet dress trimmed in white, black buttons down the center. White tights and black flats completed her look.

As the couple walked closer, Lila felt waves of hostility rolling off them. They took a seat opposite each other on the guest stools.

The audience and Mr. and Mrs. Claus looked expectantly at her.

Lila's face heated with embarrassment and her voice caught in her throat.

Ultimate stage fright.

The producer, standing behind the cameraman, waved his arms and pointed to the cards in her hands.

Oh, the cards! Thank God for the cards.

"Ah," she cleared her throat. "Welcome Terrance" — Santa's first name was Terrance?— "and Candy Claus. Thank you for joining us today."

"I wouldn't be here if it wasn't for that woman!" Mr. Claus thundered.

The audience gasped.

Lila gaped. Santa didn't act that way!

"You left me no choice!" Mrs. Claus retorted. "Toys, toys, toys! That's all it is with you."

They glared at each other.

The producer pointed at Lila.

She sifted through the cards, looking for help.

All the cards besides the top one she'd already used were empty.

Great.

"Well, Christmas is ten days away," she gently reminded Mrs. Claus.

Mrs. Claus snorted. "That means absolutely nothing. All year, every day, it's toys. Toys and more toys. He has to make them, has to try them. He has to make sure they're appropriate for each person. I want to go on vacation and he says no. He's too busy. Then he gets mad when I take matters into my own hands. A woman has to look after herself." She pointed at Lila. "Don't you forget it. Don't depend on any man."

"Ah, well," Lila stuttered. During her time in The Maze, she'd learned her love life had been sucking because of her, not her ex-boyfriends. She wasn't the best person to be giving advice.

"Those toys do need testing. I need to make sure they work before I give them away."

"Yes," Mrs. Claus agreed bitterly. "But every single one?"

"You're out of line," Mr. Claus shouted, grabbing his white and red hat and throwing it on the floor.

It landed on the carpet without making a sound, but Lila could have heard a pin drop in the studio. No one thought of Santa Claus and an angry man being one and the same.

"Oh, I don't think so," Mrs. Claus said smugly, smiling at the audience which was mainly female. "I put a camera in your toy room. I've seen what you do."

A current of anticipation zinged through the room.

Lila had to admit she wanted to see the video, too. She sat sideways in her chair for a better view of the huge screen behind her. The lights dimmed and the film began to play.

Mrs. Claus sat in the dark, an interviewer out of camera range spoke to her.

"So, Mrs. Claus, when your husband, Mr. Claus, kept giving you excuses as to why he didn't want to go on vacation, why he was so busy, what did you do?"

The Mrs. Claus on the screen played to the camera and the audience, her chin wobbling, her voice squeaky with unshed tears. "I had to know what was so important. I had to see for myself why Terrance didn't want to leave his toy workshop. So I put a camera in his room. I know it was an invasion of privacy, but a woman needs to know. What I found was shocking. Just shocking."

"Do you want the rest of the world to see what kind of man you married?" the interviewer whispered.

"Yes!" Mrs. Claus agreed firmly. "Yes. I want everyone to see what I've been unknowingly living with all these years."

The animosity of the audience toward Mr. Claus reached an apex, and Lila was afraid the room would explode if the interviewer didn't get on with it.

"All right, Mrs. Claus." The interviewer's voice oozed sympathy. "Roll the film," he demanded, and Mrs. Claus faded to black. Suddenly, a "Ho, ho, ho!" filled the room and on the large screen three women with long hair and perfect bodies in various stages of undress were kneeling on a huge bed covered with red satin sheets.

The audience gasped and a few catcalls rang out.

Santa entered the frame then, his red pants low on his hips. He wasn't wearing a shirt and his "bowl full of jelly" stomach was proudly on display, swaying in time to his foot-steps. "Ho, ho, ho!"

(That's what the "ho, ho, hos" meant all this time!)

The Santa on screen thundered again cheerfully, and he opened the cardboard box he was holding, showing a wide range of toys.

Lila had been in an adult bookstore only once and it had been enough.

Santa pulled out a big—

Lila made a slashing motion to her neck at the producer. He said something into his microphone and the screen went black.

The lights came on in the studio while the audience booed and hissed in disappointment.

Apparently everyone was in the mood for a little holiday porn this Christmas.

"Do you see what I mean now?" Mrs. Claus asked. "How can I live this way?"

"It's your fault!" Mr. Claus accused.

"No way!" Lila said, coming to Mrs. Claus's defense.

Mrs. Claus smiled at her and rubbed Lila's arm. "Thank you."

"You women taking each other's sides. It's all that baking you do. Cookies and bars and cheesecakes. Brownies. Chocolate everywhere."

Mrs. Claus' face trembled with rage. "I'm Mrs. Claus. I bake for all your goddamned elves!"

Lila winced at the expletive. Mrs. Claus' swearing wasn't very jolly.

"That's not all you do for them!"

The audience, who had been quiet during the heated exchange, started hooting and shouting.

Lila buried her face in her hands. Santa wasn't the only one who'd been naughty.

"I took pictures, myself!" Santa roared, jerking his thumb at his chest causing his eyeglasses to go askew.

"You what?" Mrs. Claus yelled.

"Oh, yes! That Caribbean holiday you took? I wondered where half my elves went."

"I didn't want to go alone!" She appealed to Lila. "You wouldn't have wanted to go on holiday alone, would you?"

Being alone right now on the beach would be a dream come true. Aqua blue waters, white sand, frozen drinks with little umbrellas, yeah, she could handle that alone just fine.

Unless Ben was with her.

She pictured them frolicking in the surf, the bright sun beating down on them. Okay, so maybe she couldn't blame Mrs. Claus after all.

The audience started chanting, "Pictures! Pictures! Pictures!" and stomping their feet.

"I suppose we have pictures," Lila said to no one.

Of course they did.

The lights in the studio lowered again and Santa appeared on the screen, definitely looking like he contained not one ounce of holiday cheer.

"What made you decide to follow your wife to the beach?" the off-screen interviewer asked Santa.

To Lila's surprise, Santa's eyes filled with tears and he drew his lips into a tight white line.

"She'd been making noises about going someplace warmer. The North Pole was too cold for her, she was getting tired of the snow."

That was a thought Lila could get behind one hundred percent.

"I was too busy to take a holiday."

"Yes! We all know why!" Mrs. Claus exclaimed over the filmed interview.

The women in the audience clapped supportively.

"But she was determined to go, so I followed her," the on-screen Santa continued. "This is what I found."

The interviewer didn't say any more.

A slideshow of pictures started, one more ludicrous than the one before.

Mrs. Claus in a red bikini (hey, she had a nice body under that thick dress!), dancing in the waves on an empty beach. Well, empty besides a group of elves wearing nothing but board shorts and green and red hats with jingle bells attached to the long pointy ends.

The next picture showed Mrs. Claus lying on a lounge chair, an elf feeding her grapes.

The next was of Mrs. Claus getting rubbed down by an elf holding a bottle of suntan oil.

The pictures turned naughtier and Lila rested her forehead on the back of her stool.

Mrs. Claus liked threesomes.

With elves.

That was so not right.

The lights came up. No one in the audience said one thing.

The producer pointed at her, but Lila was at a loss for words. In fact, it was time to get out of there.

"I'm, ah, a little out of my depth here," she admitted. "Can't you, ah, agree to disagree and go your separate ways?"

"You don't think we should fight for our marriage?" Mrs. Claus asked.

"Well, ah . . . that's not up to me," Lila told the woman honestly. "If you still love each other, if you can look past what each of you has done to the other, then yes, I suppose, but it would take a lot of work."

That's what her Grandma Jean said, too. Relationships were work, and you had to fight for what you wanted.

She wanted Ben. He was the only man she'd ever wanted, and he made her understand he was worth fighting for when he left her behind at her brother's bar.

"You would both have to give up your toys and start playing with each other." Lila slapped a hand over her mouth. That didn't come out right.

But it made Santa laugh, the huge belly laugh he was known for.

"I think Lila has a point," he admitted, sliding off the stool and taking his wife's hand.

"That she does," Mrs. Claus agreed.

Lila was relieved. Things here would be okay.

She hopped off her stool and extended her hand to her Mr. and Mrs. Claus. "Thank you for joining us," she said, then looked to her audience. "And thank you for joining us as well."

Just like that, her stage fright was gone and after a deep bow she announced, "Have a great day and thank you for stopping by the Lila Donahue Show. Free cars in the parking lot for all my guests! Merry Christmas!"

The audience rang with cheers, laughter, and tears, but Mrs. Claus was fingering the forgotten golden leash the fleas had used to keep her in line. "This is an unusual necklace. So soft, yet, is it strong?" Older woman's blue eyes were twinkling with mischief and secrets.

Lila remembered the choking sensation when the flea forced her to keep up. "Yes, it is. Why?"

"Can I have it?" Mrs. Claus asked.

189

VANIA RHEAULT

"Sure!" She didn't want any reminder of this night—
except Ben. "What will you do with it?"

Mrs. Claus loosened the knot and pulled it over Lila's
head. "I think I'll find something," she said, elbowing Mr.
Claus.

"Well, good luck."

The audience filed out of the studio with the assistance
of the producer.

The show was over.

"Oh, wait," Lila called to a departing Mr. and Mrs.
Claus. "Santa. I thought your name was Nick, you know, for
Saint Nicholas. Not Terrance."

Santa's loud voice boomed in laughter and Mrs. Claus
joined in.

"Lila, they do call him Nick. Big Nick, in fact. But not
for his stomach, if you get my meaning."

"Yes. Unfortunately, I do." Lila cringed, and shaking her
head, she approached the producer. "I need a way out of
here."

The man pointed to the far end of the room where there
was a red exit sign above a black door.

"Thanks."

Lila's heart pounded.

Where would this door lead? There wasn't any danger
here. Maybe it would be best for her to stay and wait.

No.

Grandma Jean said keeping Ben would take work. She
could spend the rest of her life being sought after by men
she didn't want, or she could take a leap of faith and start
working for what, for who, she did want. All her life she let
things drop into her lap. This time, she would go after what
she truly wanted.

Lila pushed the door open . . .

CHAPTER EIGHT

... A nd stepped into a dark alley.
Cold air bit at her face and her stockinged feet met snowy ground. She wrapped Ben's jacket closer around her. There wasn't anything she could do. She was barefoot and penniless.

To her right, the alley was a dead end. To her left, an old man hunched over a barrel, warmed by the flickering fire inside.

"Joe!" Lila called in relief.

He raised his head with a smile and his eyes met hers. "Little girl, what are you doing out here this time of night? And with no shoes?"

Lila picked her way down the alley, the snow freezing her feet.

The wind that had been so strong before had quit in the early morning hour. Now the stars were hidden by clouds and a faint glow hung in the air—lights from the city. The street was empty, and the alley was quiet but for the crackling of Joe's fire. She recognized where she was now. The door she came out of was a back door of The Maze.

Lila took a deep breath, savoring the moment, savoring her freedom. There would be no more fleas, no more strange talk shows. She would never see her grandpa get a lap dance again.

"I was trapped in The Maze," Lila said.

From a pile of garbage, Joe pulled over a large piece of cardboard, and she stood on it gratefully. She didn't care about the garbage; her feet were already dirty. She leaned over the barrel, warming her face and hands.

She knew Joe from the volunteer work she did at the church. Father Tim organized a soup kitchen on Sundays and Wednesdays. She helped him often.

"You should be getting yourself home," Joe said, peering at her across the barrel.

"I don't have any money. I left all my things in The Maze, and I can't go back in there." Can't. Won't. Wouldn't. Couldn't. It was all the same to her. She would never go in there again.

"There are still taxis out and about," Joe said. He would know with the amount of time he spent on the streets. "I'll help you. They'll wait for you to pay them once they get you home."

Lila let Joe lead her to the mouth of the alley. The road was deserted, the corner streetlight black. The time felt extremely late, or incredibly early.

Joe held out his hand, and miraculously, a yellow taxi pulled around the corner and stopped right in front of them. He opened the door for her. "Be safe, and stay out of The Maze, little girl," he said, laughing.

"That's an easy promise," Lila agreed and kissed him on his dirty cheek. "You get to the church now. It's late and it's not safe out here alone."

"I'm waiting for someone, then I'll head over."

Lila climbed into the taxi and Joe shut the door firmly behind her. She waved at him through the side window as the cab pulled away from the curb, but she didn't know if he saw her.

"Where to, lady?"

Lila shoved her hands into Ben's jacket pockets, frustrated. She didn't want to admit she didn't have money, but as she opened her mouth to tell him her address (if he wanted to get paid, he would have to wait whether he wanted to or not) her fingers curled around a wallet and a ring of keys.

A wallet.

Excitedly, Lila pulled it out. Ben's wallet. And his keys. She opened the billfold and pulled his driver's license out of the clear plastic slot.

There he was, her mind hummed happily, his picture in the little square box. A huge grin lit up his face, his eyes shining, his hair disheveled, like he had just run his fingers through it. Someone had made him laugh before the picture was taken.

That was Ben happy.

"Lady?" the cab driver prompted.

Lila met his eyes in the rear view mirror.

All her make was gone. The bright red lips, the pink blush, the bright blue eyeshadow, the drawn-in brows. It was all gone; she was back to normal. Her bangs were a mess, her hair falling, but she looked . . . normal. Tired, and normal.

Thank God Ben wouldn't see her made up like a clown.

"Lady, I can get a paying fare if you have nowhere to go."

She understood his irritation, and she must have seemed like a ditz, but after tonight, she gave herself a break.

She read Ben's address off his license and hoped he kept it updated, that she wasn't going to an address he lived at four years ago or something.

Ben's birthday was December eleventh, two weeks after hers. He had turned, she did the math, thirty-three.

She rested her head against the bench and dozed as the cabdriver wound his way through the snowy city streets.

"We're here. Fifteen bucks."

She wiped away the fog on the window and peered at the little blue house. It looked cozy and warm.

Lila slid the driver's license back into the slot and grabbed a twenty from the billfold. Ben carried a lot of cash.

The thick stack of bills reminded her of her Manolos abandoned in the woods, and she was still ticked off at Dev for making her leave them behind. She hoped she never saw him again because she kind of wanted to slap him.

"Here." She gave the cab driver the twenty and stepped from the car.

She prayed she wasn't making a big mistake.

Her feet were frozen, the cold concrete of the steps burning like fire. She hopped from one foot to the other, but it made trying all the keys on his keyring, searching for the right one, impossible. She was almost crying from pain by the time she was able to open the door. She didn't try the garage or look for a back door. She was too cold.

The doorway opened into a warm mudroom, a washer and dryer in one corner, a litter box near them on the floor.

From the doorway a black kitten stared at her with wide grey eyes, then darted away.

"Ben?" she called out, following the kitten into a spacious kitchen.

He didn't answer, and the house felt empty.

She pulled out Ben's wallet and keys and threw them

onto the table. He would be relieved they hadn't been lost. After she pulled off his jacket, she felt oddly bereft without it, and after only a couple seconds without it, she missed the brush of the collar along her jaw.

She rifled through his kitchen searching for coffee. There was a coffeemaker on the counter, there had to be grounds somewhere. As she moved, the kitten played with the ends of her dress's bow.

She must look a mess.

Lila found coffee and started a pot. The hot liquid would help warm her and the caffeine would keep her awake. She didn't want him to find her sleeping if she needed to make a hasty escape.

This whole night had been one big nightmare, and at this point, she didn't know what was real and what was fake. She was halfway in love with him, but that didn't mean he felt the same way about her.

She poured a cup of coffee, sipping it black as he didn't have milk in his refrigerator, and she sat at the table. One by one she pulled the bobby pins out of what remained of her updo and ran her fingers through her snarls. Rubbing her fingers over her scalp felt divine and made her even more tired.

White tea lights sat in the middle of the table, and she lit them using the small box of matches located conveniently near them.

With the kitten playing at her feet, and her hands wrapped around her coffee mug, she settled in to wait.

CHAPTER NINE

She didn't hear the car pull up.

Only the turn of the front door's doorknob pulled her from her sleepy silence.

She didn't know what she should do, or what she should say, so she waited nervously, wrapped her hands around her mug to keep them from shaking.

The door shut and shoes thumped on the floor of the mudroom. There was a rustling of fabric.

Ben stopped in the doorway of his kitchen and stared at her.

Lila swallowed a lump in her throat and prayed this hadn't been a mistake.

"How did you get in?"

Crap. Maybe this wasn't going to go as well as she hoped, but man, he looked good. His hair was messy, he'd lost his tie bar somewhere along the way, and he'd taken his suit coat off when he came inside. His eyelids drooped in exhaustion, and his whiskers were thicker than when she had met him at The Lucky Clover.

Lila dangled his keys. She didn't trust herself to speak; she might burst into tears instead.

"But how did you know where I live?" he insisted.

Maybe he was having a hard time processing what had happened, too. If he cared about her like he said he did in the tunnel, maybe this whole thing felt like another room in The Maze.

Keeping her cool, she tilted her head toward his wallet on the table. "I found your driver's license. I hope you don't mind." I hope you don't mind? God, it was more than that. She hoped he was happy, she hoped he was damn ecstatic she tracked him down. She hoped he was madly in love with her. But then she remembered the pilfered twenty and frowned. "I paid for a taxi with some cash from your wallet. I didn't know what else to do. I never made it back to the coat check to grab my jacket. I can pay you back."

Ben finally took a step toward her and said, "I don't mind. You don't have to pay me back. Lila, you could have gone home."

She couldn't have gone home. All she wanted from the minute she met him was to take care of him, make sure he would be okay. Then after The Maze, she couldn't imagine life without him. She stood and took a step toward him too, her heart in her throat. "I didn't want to go home. I wanted to see you." She was going to cry.

She'd made it through the whole night, Dev, the fleas, seeing her grandma, the talk show, without breaking down, but now in Ben's kitchen, with him being so close, yet so far, she was going to cry. "Oh, God, Ben, I was so worried about you. Wh-what happened to you after the train?"

"Nothing I want to talk about now. Lila, you're okay?"

Ben picked her up and sat her on the island. They were

as close as they had been in her brother's bar, and she look into his eyes. His touch was familiar, his voice the same.

This was Ben; she'd missed him desperately.

She nodded, and he studied her face, as if making sure she was telling the truth. But she was. She was all right. She was now, anyway.

Lila pulled on his tie, pressed her lips to his, and she leaned in when he cupped her face in his hands.

He pulled her closer, and in relief and happiness, she wrapped her arms around his neck.

She was disappointed when he broke the kiss, but they were both exhausted, they were both filthy from walking through the woods, and probably neither of them wanted to admit how unreal this all felt.

"Are you tired, sweetheart?"

Oh, he called her sweetheart.

Her heart landed at his feet.

Completely in love, she rested her head against his shoulder. "Yeah, I am. Can I stay?"

Oh please let me stay.

Ben picked her up and cradled her against his chest, the exact same way he carried her through the woods. With a smile, she wondered if that's why he hadn't wanted to put her down. He was being a gentleman, helpful, his knight to her damsel, but maybe he wanted her close because he was falling in love too. The thought made joy bloom in her heart and she didn't think she could be any happier than when he told her, "You can stay, Lila. You can stay, for the rest of your life, if you'd like."

She didn't say anything, scared she would burst into tears, and she pressed her lips together as he walked her up to his bedroom and laid her down on the bed. Gently, he pulled a blanket that was folded at the end over her and he climbed in beside her.

Lila rolled on her side and grabbed his hand. She tucked it under her cheek, loath to break contact, even in sleep.

As she drifted off, she knew things would be all right. She would have to thank Brigid later, for making them go to The Maze, because thanks to her, she had found Ben on the corner of Hamilton and Main.

EPILOGUE

"It still seems like a dream sometimes."

"I don't know what else it could have been."

After visiting with Danny, they walked downtown, toward The Maze. They'd told him the happy news: they were engaged.

Winter had finally gone and a warm breeze blew through her hair. Ben squeezed her hand and the unfamiliar pressure of her engagement ring made her giggle. She was so happy.

She never told Ben what happened to her after the train, and he'd told her only bits and pieces of his night: the poker game, the hospital, Joe helping him to the church, meeting Father Tim. She didn't want to tell him about the fleas, or speak about her grandmother. Not yet. Maybe, after their lives settled down, she would tell him those things, and about Santa and Mrs. Claus. Christmas would never be the same for her again.

She was relieved when they found out his friends had also escaped The Maze, and she was happy for him he'd made peace with Felix.

Lila had also been a little dumbfounded to learn Simon of the infamous smoke bombs was Ben's friend, and she made him promise to leave his smoke bombs at home during their wedding reception. They were planning their wedding now, and his friends were a part of it.

Her friends didn't speak of their time in The Maze, either, and it was just as well. They had gotten out safely, and that was all that mattered in the end.

Brigid married days before Christmas in a beautiful ceremony. Lila was maid of honor, and Ben was her date. Brigid said she'd happily return the favor.

Now, she wanted to see The Maze one last time, so she asked Ben to walk with her. They stood on the corner, the old grey stone building looking a bit worse for wear, and she leaned against the light pole. "We can't hate the place."

Ben rested his arm above her head and palmed her cheek. She couldn't believe how much she loved this man, and him, her. Without talking to her Grandma Jean that night in The Maze, she may never have had the courage to go after him, to go after what she wanted. He said he would've asked for her at Danny's bar, and her heart warmed when she thought of it. But it made her happy she'd taken that first step to further their relationship. It made them even—they were both invested. Whole-heartedly.

"No," he agreed, "I'll never truly hate it, because it brought me to you, but I'll never go in there again."

He bent to kiss her, and she met his lips eagerly.

"But there is one thing I keep forgetting to ask since that night."

Lila's heart thudded in her chest. She wasn't sure she was up to answering any questions, but she asked lightly, "Oh, yeah? What's that?"

"How did you walk across the floor grating in your high heels?"

That was the last question Lila expected, and she laughed. She didn't have the answer, so she kissed him and said, "It must have been magic."

That's what it felt like to her. A fairy tale.

And they would live happily ever after.

A NOTE FROM THE AUTHOR

First books are hard. And with the invention of self-publishing, a lot, if not most, first books aren't shoved under beds like they're supposed to be, but put out into the world.

Some first books are amazing, and their authors hit it out of the park their first time out. But the majority of writers can't do that, and what happens is the book market is flooded with mediocre books.

I thought *The Corner of 1700 Hamilton* wasn't like other first books. I hired people to edit it, and I asked for a lot of feedback. But the problem is, editors and feedback only slightly help with the writing process, and it's obvious after editing these novellas that I'm far ahead of where I was four years ago in terms of craft and skill. (What does help? Writing. Lots of writing.)

That doesn't change the fact that for four years I had a mediocre book out there with my name on it.

Because this time in our lives will always be remembered as the year the COVID-19 pandemic swept the world, the decision to re-edit this book was a was an easy one. With so much going on it was hard to focus, but I still wanted to be productive.

Under all the stiff writing and telling and not showing, I believed these two novellas had something to offer, and I took time out of my writing schedule to go back and revisit Ben and Lila.

I hope I cleaned the dirt off these gems, and now readers can enjoy them as they were meant to be.

A writer's path should always be moving forward, but that doesn't mean we forget about the accomplishments in our past.

Books never die, and now I have a cleaner, better, version of mine.

Please enjoy! And if you did, drop me a line telling me so. I appreciate it. Stay safe and well!

Vania Rheault

ACKNOWLEDGMENTS

Thank you to Liz at thewritingreader.com/blog. Without her fantastic writing prompts there wouldn't be a tunnel scene. Thanks for all your support and enthusiasm!

Thanks to everyone who proofed and edited *1700 Hamilton*:

Kay Gardner

Jewel E. Leonard

David Willis

Thomas Jast

Joshua Edward Smith

Thanks to everyone who proofed and edited *On the Corner of Hamilton and Main*:

Jewel E. Leonard

Thomas Jast

Joshua Edward Smith

ABOUT THE AUTHOR

Vania Rheault is an avid reader and has been writing from a young age. Always with a cup of coffee in hand, she enjoys the seasons in Minnesota with her two children, and two cats. *The Corner of 1700 Hamilton* was her first book, and since then she's settled into the contemporary romance genre.

Visit her at vaniamargene.com and these other social media outlets.

www.ingramcontent.com/pod-product-compliance
Lightning Source LLC
Chambersburg PA
CBHW022058170626
46808CB00002B/497